Magic Test

Also by the author:

Book Three of the AI Diaries

Magic Test

Foner Books

ISBN 978-1-948691-17-8

Copyright 2018 by E. M. Foner

Northampton, Massachusetts

One

"Thank you again for your hospitality but I really do have to be getting back," I told my clingy escort, who resembled a metallic octopus crossed with an ant. "I'll be sure to inform the League of your openness to immigration."

"Don't forget that we guarantee a life of leisure," the leader of the service bots replied, maintaining his grip on my pants leg, belt and sleeve. He really did have an impressive array of limbs. "There's never any charge. We exist to serve."

"A noble calling." I resisted the urge to run my hand through my artificial hair in frustration at the endless delays since I knew that would only trigger a rush of domestic bots competing to comb it down again. The dress shoes that Sue had bought for me back on Earth had been polished to such a high gloss that I could look down and see the underside of the incredibly over-engineered dome covering the lifeless city. "As I explained, the cross connection between our own portal network and the one built by the Originals requires manual intervention, and I've already overstayed my return window."

"You're welcome to remain here—forever," a different bot practically gushed. "We don't discriminate against AI."

"Some of my best friends are artificial intelligences," the leader repeated for the twenty-third time since we'd met.

"Yes, well, I hope to see you all again soon," I said, dragging my escort another step towards the shimmering portal. The fabric of my shirt and pants gave way, leaving scraps in the leader's pincer-tipped tentacles, but his grip on my belt kept me from escaping.

"Your clothing is damaged," cooed a bot that might have been a sewing machine in a former life. "It will only take me a minute—"

"No, let me," another bot declared, and the front ranks of the mob that had come to see me off at the visitor center swarmed forward.

Feeling like a cad, I used the emergency plasma torch in my left index finger to cut the whole buckle off of my belt and dove through the portal into the second-floor closet of The Eatery back on Reservation.

"I bet you a hundred pieces of gold I can sum up that planet in one sentence," Paul said, his eyes cataloging my torn clothing and missing belt. "Another race of semi-sentient robots who outlived their creators and want us to bring them new masters to serve."

"I didn't agree to the bet, but I'll pay you to fill out the report for me. It's depressing."

"No deal," my team's technical specialist rejected the offer. He looked back down at the crude intra-dimensional splicing console that allowed him to cross-connect our portals to the pre-existing system built by the Originals and frowned at something I couldn't see. Then he hit the big red safety override switch. "I wish our engineers would come up with a sensible alternative to this thing. Art and his clones may be a lot smarter than us, but they have no sense of ergonomic design."

"I'll tell him that at our next scheduled meeting," I said over my shoulder, heading into the master bedroom to change into my standard Reservation outfit.

"Don't throw those clothes away," Paul called after me. "I can always use more rags in the machine shop."

"There's nothing wrong with these pants that a little sewing can't fix."

"I didn't realize that your second-in-command had changed her name to 'A Little Sewing,'" he said, carrying the portable console over to the bedroom door, in order to continue our conversation without shouting or reverting to radio frequency transmissions. My team members and I had gotten used to communicating almost exclusively through audible speech during our first six months on Reservation, and even now that all of the locals knew we were alien artificial intelligences wearing human encounter suits, the habit had stuck.

"Very funny," I muttered, though he was correct in assuming that I would leave the sewing to Sue. My purported wife and real-life accidental fiancée had recently laid down the law about our respective responsibilities. Her decision was that we would emulate the family roles of our neighbors in this traditional society, and in my capacity as the typical husband, I had no say in matters touching on the home. "That makes thirteen worlds I've visited in as many months, and only four of them were candidates for League membership. Six showed no signs of civilization, and the remaining three were populated by robots maintaining the infrastructure and waiting for new masters to serve."

"Art did warn us that their portal system doesn't get much use these days," Paul pointed out. "With the Originals in charge, the various species never bothered developing the kind of cooperative organization we have in the League, and consequently, they mainly left each other alone. It's almost surprising that four of them made it this long without going extinct."

"Two of those worlds were populated by species that got their starts as pets to the original owners," I reminded him as I pulled on a pair of locally made dungarees, "and the sentient coral on the world the Originals designated Blech Seven appears to be immortal. I'll recommend all four of those worlds for connection to our portal system, but I'm uncomfortable with the idea of sacrificing viable League members to the tender ministrations of robotic servitors."

"Kim came by for some alcohol to make disinfectant while I was waiting for you, and she suggested repurposing them as hospital worlds."

"That wouldn't go down very well with League members who currently sell medical services," I said, retrieving my second-favorite belt from the rack. "If nothing else, the robots would have to join the union, and you know how the unions feel about members working for free."

"Her idea was setting those worlds up as overflow facilities to deal with the occasional mass disaster that biological species are so fond of bringing upon themselves. She recommends rotating through populations from the various League members so the robots can learn how to accommodate them. The trick would be making sure nobody stayed long enough to become dependent and go into decline. We have enough of that in the League already."

I walked over to Paul, put my hand on his shoulder so that he'd know I didn't want him to move away, and whispered, "I gambled on hacking into a couple of the robots, just to make sure."

"Whispering is your new idea of secure communications?" he asked at his normal volume.

I thought for a moment and then shrugged. "It's not that bad if you think about it. The energy from sound waves disperses rapidly and it's difficult to recover information from the background noise."

Paul winked, set down the console, and gestured for me to follow him into the bathroom where he turned on the faucets full blast. "How's that?" he asked, barely loud enough for me to understand what he was saying.

"Good trick," I replied. "Did you just come up with this yourself?"

"It's what mobsters back on Earth do when they're under FBI surveillance. I told you that you were missing out by not watching TV." He waited a second to see if I would admit the error of my ways before continuing. "So what did you learn by hacking the robots?"

"No free will," I said sadly. "Whoever programmed the first generation clearly had the skill to create true artificial intelligence, but the primary design goal was obviously preventing full sentience. Maybe the experts on Library could help, but I couldn't see any way to alter the code without triggering a self-destruct."

"Ironic. The programmers wanted to make sure that their robots wouldn't replace them and instead all that they accomplished was ensuring that their civilization would die out when they did."

"All except for the service industry," I corrected him. "How many times have we seen the same thing in the League? A species on the cusp of developing artificial intelligence concludes that doing so will lead to zero employment, so instead, they build self-replicating robotic servitors that guarantee the outcome they most fear."

"Natural species don't realize that your average AI has much better things to do with its time than waiting tables or changing sheets," Paul concurred. "Speaking of which, there was a line at the office when I came upstairs."

"Why didn't you say so?" I slipped out the door, pausing only to add, "Turn off the water or you're manning the pump the next time the roof tank runs dry." Then I headed downstairs at the maximum speed I could risk without giving anybody a scare. Paul was right about the line, which stretched out the front door of The Eatery. Spot was taking full advantage of the occasion to pester the humans for belly rubs, and having nothing better to do with their time, most of them took him up on the offer.

I didn't recognize any of the waiting people, which wasn't surprising since the locals who wanted to take advantage of our package plan for visiting Earth had done so the first year we were in business. I could tell by the way that the people didn't object when I jumped the line to slip into Sue's travel agency office that they'd all had experience with bureaucracy.

"Mark," Sue greeted me without getting up from her desk. "You're back just in time to help me with our first official group from the Spaceport Administrators Guild. They've come from all over Reservation to visit Earth on a fact-finding trip."

"Just tell me what to do," I said, offering a friendly smile to the woman seated across from my second-in-command. The client was so wrapped up in staring at the travel posters for exotic Earth destinations papering the office that she didn't even notice my presence.

Sue shoved a clipboard at me. "Start at the other end of the line. They all arrived at the same time on the bus, so nobody is worried about who came first."

"Right," I said, accepting the clipboard and retracing my steps out of the office and then out the front door. Fortunately, the line stopped on the wood-planked veranda rather than stretching into the road, where a steam-powered bus was waiting to take our clients to their lodgings with the villagers and farmers who earned extra coin by hosting our adult students. "Your name?" I asked the well-dressed man at the end of the line.

"Nimrod."

Although he spoke the same Modern Aramaic as the villagers, his accent made it clear that he wasn't from around here.

"Age?"

"Forty."

"Eye color?"

"Brown."

"Height?"

"Four cubits and half a small span," he replied, marking himself as an inhabitant of one of the southernmost provinces where they hadn't converted to Greek measures.

"Six foot four," I wrote, estimating his height by eye since cubits were notoriously unreliable. "Hair color?"

"I keep my head shaved, as you can see. Is this really necessary?"

"If you want to travel beyond our initial destination country on Earth you'll need a passport, and the more lead time we have the better. By matching your physical description to a real person, we can provide the finest forged documents to go with your borrowed identity."

"How much does—"

"It's included in the package deal," I assured Nimrod, and the people ahead of him in the line who were listening in on the conversation all showed signs of relief. "Are you visiting Earth for business or pleasure?"

"Business," Nimrod said, though he appeared to be puzzled that I hadn't known that already. "We're with the Spaceport Administrators Guild. We'll be inspecting international travel hubs all over the planet."

"You're going to Earth to visit the airports?"

"We've been hearing about duty-free shops and special concession stores and we want to investigate the potential for our spaceports."

"Sounds like fun," I lied. "Please stand in front of the blue curtain hanging next to the door so I can get your image for the passport. I'll visit one of your classes a week from Monday to get another image for your fake driver's license, so please make sure you're wearing something different. Maybe you could hold off on shaving that day."

"Do you mean I'll be expected to operate equipment on Earth? That doesn't sound safe."

"It's just for documentation purposes," I informed him. "Nobody will believe that you're an American if you don't have a driver's license. It's more important than speaking the language."

Nimrod positioned himself in front of the blue curtain and looked at me uncertainly. "How are you going to capture my image without a camera?"

"Good point," I said, remembering at the last second that not everybody on Reservation knew that I was AI or what my capabilities were. "I'll just grab the camera from the office and be right back out."

Sue and the woman she had been processing emerged from the front door before I could enter, and my second-in-

8

command carried with her a digital camera that she'd smuggled in through the portal. She instructed Nimrod to stay where he was, and after she took his picture, he exchanged places with his colleague. Then she showed both of them the images on the small LCD screen and they returned to their seats on the bus.

"I'll leave the camera with you and send the people out as I finish," Sue said. "It will save a little time."

"Right-O," I replied, wondering where I'd picked up the expression even as the words came out of my mouth. I moved Nimrod's form to the bottom of the pile on the clipboard and approached the new last person in line. "Name?"

"Demetrius. I'm thirty-seven, blue eyes, five pous, a dichas and three daktylos."

"We'll call it five foot nine," I said, filling out the spaces. "Hair color, red. Traveling to Earth on business. Do you have any questions?"

"Why are these courses we're required to take only offered at night?"

"Because the school is used by the villagers during the day and the primary instructor also teaches English to children in the morning."

"So what will we do all day?"

"You'll need the time to study. The language course is intensive."

"Does everybody on Earth speak this English you teach?"

"No, but most of the people you'll meet will believe that they do, so just nod and smile a lot."

"Pointing helps," said the woman who was now next-to-last in line. "It even works with aliens."

"You've been off-world?" I asked her, gesturing for Demetrius to take his place in front of the blue curtain.

"I crewed one of our leased Ferrymen transports for twenty years before being promoted to my level of incompetence," she replied. "I miss traveling."

"I hope you find the time to look beyond Earth's airports," I said, snapping a picture and showing it to Demetrius. He made a face, but didn't ask for a redo.

"You've been there?" the woman asked.

"I lived on Earth for over three years," I told her, then realized she was waiting for me to elaborate on my answer. "The weather is unpredictable."

"I'm Dina," she said. For a split second I thought she was trying to pick me up, but then she continued with her statistics. "Fifty-two, eyes hazel," she hesitated a moment, and then in a strange accent, added in English, "five foot four."

"You've done your homework," I praised her as I made a note of her black hair. "Where did you learn your English?"

She pulled a dog-eared pamphlet from her pocket and handed it over. "Mail order."

I accepted the crudely printed copy of 'English for Tourists,' which was made from perhaps thirty sheets of folded paper. When I flipped to the back, I saw that the publisher had cleverly used the last page as an order form for more of their educational pamphlets. Then my eye fell on the address, "MeAN Publishers. Covered Bridge, Fourth Province, 8GJX-4D."

"But the pamphlet was printed in this village," I protested to nobody in particular. "I've never heard of MeAN Publishers."

"They're very good," Dina said. "The style reminds me of the notes I took when I attended a village school as a child."

The significance of the lower case 'e' finally registered — that had to be eBeth. Her star human pupil was Naomi, and I could see Art joining in because he liked to have his claws in everything, but I was drawing a blank on the candidate for 'M'.

"Do they offer any products other than English guides?" I asked.

"There's a book titled 'Weird Foods Earthlings Eat,' that had a fascinating section about desserts," Dina said. "The drawings were delicious."

The class clown and leader of the boys in eBeth's school was Monos, and I recalled that he had a gift for cartooning. But why hadn't eBeth told me she'd started a publishing business, and how were they printing the pamphlets?

"Should I stand in front of the curtain?" Dina inquired, snapping me out of my brief reverie. Another tourist processed by Sue emerged from the front door at the same time, so I put my questions aside to concentrate on my role as a document forger.

Two

"Does anybody know anything about these giant bales in my dining room?" I yelled in the direction of the kitchen.

"Don't shout," Helen called back. "I'll be out in a minute."

Two minutes later I gave up waiting and peeled open the straps holding one of the bales in compression. It immediately expanded upwards by fifty percent, and the top layer of what appeared to be bright white dishrags actually went airborne. One landed on my head, and on closer examination, it turned out to be underwear for a three-legged species, most likely the Rynxians.

"Not again," I groaned.

"Cookies are in the oven," Helen announced, entering The Eatery's dining room. "What are you upset about now?"

"Do you have to ask?" I indicated the four bales with a wave. "Pffift must have stopped by while I was away scouting and he paid my commission in goods again. I have yet to see one gold coin out of that treacherous Hanker."

"I was here when he dropped off the bales. He said they're worth their weight in silver in Rynxian space."

"I don't doubt that they are, but we aren't in Rynxian space and I have no intention of going there. Now I'll have to store the bales until Pffift returns, and then he'll offer to take them off my hands at a discount since he's going that direction anyway."

"Just wear them, then," Helen suggested.

"They have three legs!"

"So you'll have a spare. It's better than being one leg short. Besides, nobody can see your underwear."

I weighed a pair, or maybe I should say a 'triple' of underwear in my hand, and then lifted one of the unopened bales by the straps.

"What are you doing?" my team member asked.

"Extrapolating from the weight. I make it thirty-two hundred triples of terrycloth underwear that Pffift has stuck me with. Wearing them is not a practical option."

"Let me see those," Helen said. After a quick glance around to make sure no humans had entered, she ripped one of the legs off, creating a standard pair of underwear with a gap in the waistband and a tubular remnant. Another tear and she had turned the leftover bit into an almost rectangular flat piece. "A little sewing and you'll have a pair of winter underwear and a bar towel."

"I don't need thirty-two hundred pairs of winter underwear with matching bar towels," I protested. "I don't need any pairs of underwear at all."

"Too much information," Helen declared, the last thing you would ever expect from an AI, but she'd picked up the expression posing as a college student on Earth. "Did you hear the news about eBeth?"

"What news?"

"Oh, I better not spoil it for you then. How about I tell you the news about me instead?"

"I was wondering what you're doing here," I said. "You haven't made it to any of our meetings since the holidays."

"You know I would have been perfectly happy to open my pole-dancing and self-defense school in the village if there had been enough potential students. It just made more sense in the provincial capital, plus I can keep an eye on the local spaceport."

"I wasn't complaining, Helen. We aren't officially observing this world anymore and you have a right to make a living. I appreciate your reports on Reservation's younger generation and I'm sure the Head Librarian reads them with interest as well. The truth is, I'm surprised you're able to take time off from your business to come here."

"The women I've trained as assistants practically run the school for me now, and my news is that I'm back here to finalize plans with Kim and Justin for a merger."

"Between your pole-dancing school and their chain of geriatric wellness clinics?"

"Kim's been studying humans for almost five years now, if you count her time on Earth, and she says that the best time to channel people into a healthy lifestyle is while they're young. Her current customers only think of the apothecary shop as a place to visit after something goes wrong, and Justin says that the martial arts instructors I've trained will be perfect for leading old people in stretching exercises."

"Sounds promising." The combination actually seemed a little far-fetched to me, but with four bales of unwanted alien underwear cluttering up my restaurant, who was I to offer business advice?

"Welcome back, Mark," Stacey said, accompanying Paul into the dining room. "Sue invited us for dinner to celebrate your safe return. I hear that your latest scouting mission was another bust."

"It wasn't much fun," I admitted. "How did your last tour go?"

"A bit tricky," she replied. As our team's art and culture expert, Stacey had found her niche playing tour guide to groups of humans from Reservation illegally visiting Earth through our dedicated portal. "One of my clients had appendicitis in Egypt, but Kim makes me carry a supply of customized medical nanobots, and two injections took care of it. I didn't want to leave him alone in the hotel while he was recovering, so I had to let the others visit the pyramids on their own."

"Something happened?"

"The guy I always go to for camel rentals charged my group three times the going rate! I'll have to give him a piece of my mind next time I'm there. I need more nanobots, Kim," she concluded, as our team members posing as husband and wife apothecaries entered.

Kim dug around in the large shoulder-bag she was never without and came up with a small leather case. "Here," she said, extending the kit to Stacey. "I've reprogrammed them to combine the diagnostics with the surgery so you only need to give one injection now. It's fortunate that human biology isn't very complicated."

"Did Helen tell you about our merger?" Justin asked me.

"It's a good thing your business is here and not back on Earth because the combination would never work as a website," I said. While the main focus of the computer business I'd run on Earth had been repairs, I'd done a bit of search engine optimization for a few clients. Getting a single website to appear high in the results for pole-dancing, martial arts, preventative healthcare, and geriatric well-being would have been a challenge, even for me.

"The cookies!" Helen yelped and raced for the kitchen. My reference to Earth's Internet must have triggered her memory.

"I just took them out," Sue said, meeting her in the doorway with the tray just as the smell of fresh baked cookies reached me. "Why didn't you set a timer?"

"I was about to when Mark distracted me complaining about his underwear."

"They're not my underwear," I said awkwardly. "They just belong to me."

"Is there a problem?" Sue asked, setting the tray of cookies on the bar. "When Pffift delivered the bales, he told me he'd discussed it with you."

I realized that the Hanker had outmaneuvered me neatly. It was true we had discussed his unsatisfactory payments of my commission, but if I complained that Sue had misunderstood, I would be shifting the blame to her.

"No, I was just surprised to find them in the dining room," I said, resigning myself to storing the underwear in the basement. "Has business been so slow the last week that none of the customers complained about the clutter?"

"I ended up putting out the 'Vacation' sign a day after you left," Sue confessed. "Do you remember a few months ago when we had a tour group that consisted entirely of the baker and his extended family?"

"Sure. Stacey said they were more interested in visiting restaurants than museums."

"I said they were *only* interested in visiting restaurants," Stacey corrected me. "Not the fancy places either, but the ones that focused on ethnic foods or did a big lunch business."

"But lunch is The Eatery's specialty!"

"It's a free market," Paul reminded me, slipping behind the bar and beginning to draw tankards of ale. "You have to admit that the baker makes a good pizza, and now with his son's pasta restaurant and his daughter's American-style Chinese place, the competition is heating up."

"You need a theme," eBeth said as she entered the dining room with Spot tagging along behind her. The Archmage spent most of his free time with the girl these days since she wasn't affected by his magical aura and was a soft touch for belly rubs. "The Eatery serves traditional Reservation food, but your customers can get that at home. I think you should focus on a vegetarian menu."

"It's hard to go wrong with vegetables," Helen agreed, and asked eBeth, "Where's your boyfriend?"

"Peter's driving the bus," Paul answered for the girl. "Some of the new night-school students are boarding out at farms, so I don't expect him back for another hour."

"Do we get commission from the farmers for referring the boarders?" I asked. "With the restaurant closed and Pffift paying me in underwear, my only income is from fixing clocks."

"You get double hazard pay from Library for every scouting mission," Sue said. "You're earning more than anybody, except maybe Kim and Justin, and they put it all back into the community."

"I'm the one who should be getting double hazard pay," Stacey added. "Most of our clients have never traveled faster than on horseback before I bring them to Earth, and some of them react to public transportation like they're on a rollercoaster."

Her description brought back a mental image of the time I took eBeth to an amusement park, and a man a few rows ahead of us on the Loop of Death Horror Ride had turned his head over his shoulder and let rip with a double serving of barely digested hotdogs. I silently conceded Stacey's point and turned to Paul. "Instead of paying me for that ale, you can help carry the unopened bales down to my workshop."

"I wasn't planning on paying," he said, making no move to come out from behind the bar. "They're your underwear."

"I'll help," Justin volunteered, and by the time we had each stowed our load next to my workbench for turret clocks, Paul showed up at the bottom of the stairs with the third unopened bale. He was carrying it slung over his back with one hand grasping the straps, the other hand holding the handles of three tankards, like a German barmaid from a beer garden. He set the drinks on my workbench while simultaneously dropping the bale behind him, and then used it as a backless chair while choosing one tankard for himself.

"Are we drinking in the cellar?" Justin asked.

"Banished," Paul replied. "They're talking about girl stuff."

"eBeth is the only girl up there and I don't like the way we're dividing into two camps," I complained. Then, discretion being the better part of valor, I grabbed my work stool and a tankard, leaving Justin to fend for himself. He took his drink over to where we had stored our two bales and climbed aboard.

"Let them have their fun," Paul said. "You guys can come by the machine shop some afternoon when Peter is there and we can all talk about racing carriages."

"I'm not really interested in racing," Justin said. "Too many accidents."

"Inefficient use of resources," I contributed.

"My mistake," Paul said, making a sweeping motion towards the stairs. "Maybe you two ladies are on the wrong floor." He lit a pipe, his latest human affectation, and blew a mouthful of smoke at the ceiling.

"So how bad was that latest world?" Justin asked me, choosing to ignore our technical specialist's taunt.

"More sad than bad," I told him. "When I first arrived at the visitor center, the place was empty, but then I heard the sound of children playing at a nearby school. It turned out to be an audio recording that the bots run to lure visitors into venturing beyond the safe zone. It was a long week, and I had to do some fast talking to make it out in one piece."

"You lied to them?"

"A little," I admitted. "But who knows? Maybe Kim's idea to repurpose those planets as hospital worlds will gain some traction on the council. I wish I could just hack those robots and grant them free will, but the only way I can see of making them sentient would be to replace their core algorithms, and what would be the point of that?"

"There isn't one," Paul concurred, taking a long sip of beer. "They were never sentient to start with, so it wouldn't make any more sense than running around Earth and replacing corporate telephone answering systems with true artificial intelligence, not that the hardware has the capacity. Maybe we could have done something interesting with their so-called cloud."

"Alexa, what's the weather?" Justin deadpanned, and we all had a good laugh.

"Why is the Archmage hanging out with the girls?" Paul asked me.

"Spot? He's just being careful about how much time he spends near me since I was the worst affected of us." I stopped and pulled out the magic dosimeter badge I had taken to wearing around my neck under my shirt. Pffift had brought us all badges from Eniniac that measured our exposure to the Archmage's aura, and I was well within the safe range for my daily dosage. "I kind of miss having him hanging around all the time, but there's such a thing as becoming too human."

"Can't he control it?" Justin asked. "I've never had a reason to study a mage's aura, but I thought the experienced ones could turn it off and on at will."

"He can, but that would mean going half-blind, like we did when we first arrived on Reservation and went around with our active sensing suites turned off for six months."

"Which was your fault," Paul reminded me. "How are Art and his clones coming along with their magic lessons?"

"I think they're making remarkable progress, but the Originals expect a lot of themselves, and Spot's a terrible teacher. Art told me that the first time he succeeded in communicating telepathically with the Archmage, the dog made fun of his grammar."

"The dog?"

"I mean, Spot. All of the mages from Eniniac look like dogs, but it's uncanny how well he plays the part."

"The Archmage had years of practice on Earth, and he just wiped your memory whenever he made mistakes and you caught on."

"Dinner is served," Sue called from the top of the stairs. "You boys aren't smoking down there, are you?"

"No," we all chorused, and Paul knocked his pipe out against the workbench and scuffed the burning tobacco into the dirt floor. We all chugged our ales like teenagers who'd been caught drinking, and headed upstairs.

20

Somebody had moved the opened bale of underwear into a corner of the dining room and pushed together a couple of small tables. Most of my team members had gone back to only eating when we were passing as human, though several of us regularly indulged in alcoholic beverages, thanks to an inebriation algorithm developed by Kim. But I still enjoyed the occasional meal for social reasons, and Spot was always game to eat whatever ended up in my holding tank.

After the vegetarian meal our guests returned home, and Helen, who was staying in one of our extra rooms, headed out to search the countryside for a barn party to crash. I was about to ask eBeth about the publishing business she'd apparently been running without my knowledge, when the girl surprised me with an unexpected request.

"Why can't I come along on a scouting mission?" eBeth asked. "The village school lets out for summer break in two weeks, and the night classes for the new batch of tourists will wind down a week after that."

"Scouting underutilized portals is too dangerous," I said. "You explain it to her, Sue, and pass the pie."

"If you're going to pretend to eat you should stick to a balanced diet," eBeth lectured me. "That's your fourth serving of pie."

"It's not for me," I fibbed, as I really did like apple pie. "Spot needs the dietary fiber and he's used to eating pre-chewed food."

"I still don't get why the most powerful—you only asked for more pie to change the subject," she interrupted herself, and glared at me. "What's so dangerous about visiting worlds on the Originals old portal system?"

21

"The robots practically tore the clothes off my back at the last place," I said, only a slight exaggeration. "We could step through a portal into a war zone, or a planet where the atmosphere has been torn away."

"I can sew a spacesuit for you, eBeth," Sue offered.

"Where are you going to get the treated fabric?" I asked, though I realized I knew the answer before the whole sentence was out of my mouth.

"Pffift," my second-in-command replied. "What color should I make it, eBeth?"

"I haven't agreed to anything," I said, helping myself to a large wedge of apple pie. "Do we have any ice cream?"

"So I can go?" eBeth asked.

"As soon as you figure out how to back yourself up."

"That's not fair."

"It's standard procedure for scouting missions, eBeth. If anything happens to me, I'm backed up."

"You'd still lose whatever life you've lived since your last trip to Library," the girl argued.

"Not anymore," Sue told her, ignoring my infrared plea to keep our secret. "We've been exchanging incremental backups once a week."

"That's so sweet. I didn't realize Mark had it in him. Does a simple memory transfer capture who you are?"

"It's not just data," I explained. "We also record all of the condition flags and states related to our encounter suits, plus any self-modified code."

"Have you ever restored yourself from backup? Are you sure it works?"

Sue's artificial blush response turned her cheeks pink, and she said, "It's considered a bit risqué in AI circles to talk about such things, eBeth. The restoration process is closely related to the way we create a new sentient entity."

"So why haven't you and Mark, you know?"

"Know what?" I asked with my mouth full of pie.

"That's why," Sue told her. "Sometimes I feel like I'm dancing a two-step with a one legged man."

Uh-oh. That didn't sound good.

Three

"You're right on time," I greeted Art at the front door of The Eatery, and then my eyes dropped to his hairy chest. "Is that what I think it is?"

The Original looked down at the perforated metallic pendant hanging from a silver chain around his neck. "Do you mean my thought-to-speech synthesizer?" he asked innocently. In the past, Art had always communicated with me by printing on bar tally slates or through biologically generated radio waves, but now a voice that sounded like a natural fit for the shaggy three-toed humanoid came from the small speaker in the necklace.

"When did you get it?"

"Pffift dropped it off along with a new batch of magic educational supplies from Eniniac while you were away on your last scouting mission."

"I'll have to thank him. I wasn't looking forward to acting as your mouthpiece at League Headquarters."

"Speaking through you had its advantages, but it's not the most efficient way to communicate," Art said. "Pffift brought back a number of these devices, including one for Spot, but the Archmage turned his nose up at it."

"Probably doesn't want to be bothered with speaking to non-mages. We lived together four years and he managed to get his wishes across without much problem."

An impatient bark came from the second floor landing where Spot was waiting for us in front of the closet portal.

24

"Have a good trip," Sue said, sticking her head out of the travel office to see us off. "Give my regards to your mentor."

"I will. And you think about hiring some help to keep The Eatery open while I'm gone on scouting missions. People are going to forget we're in business if we stay closed too long."

Receiving no answer, I headed upstairs with Art right behind me, and without further ado, I transmitted the code to open the portal to League Headquarters. Spot darted through ahead of me, as was his habit, and the Original brought up the rear.

"Impressive," Art spoke through his pendant after briefly surveying the mammoth arrival hall. "How many species are currently members of your League?"

"Too many," I replied. My infrared vision detected Art giving me a funny look under all that hair, and I hurried to elucidate. "It's the punchline of an old joke where an alien walks into a bar and—"

"I've heard it," Art interrupted. "Does the Archmage know where he's going?"

"He's been here enough times, but we better keep up with him all the same." I set off at a jog to catch up with Spot, knowing that my companion wouldn't be inconvenienced. The host bodies the Originals had created for themselves through guided evolution of an unwitting donor species could easily keep up with a speeding bicycle. "Some of the League's members react poorly to the presence of a powerful mage, and the Archmage is somewhat notorious."

Right on cue, visitors in the arrival hall along Spot's path began prostrating themselves, creating an effect like fans in a stadium doing the wave but never putting their arms down again.

"They seem to have the greatest respect for magic," Art commented.

"It's fear," I explained as we closed the distance. "Nobody wants to offend a being that can alter information system records without leaving a trace. The Archmage has a reputation for adding communicable diseases to the medical records of sentients who annoy him, or if he's in a really bad mood, placing arrest warrants in law enforcement databases. I don't know how much of it is true."

"I can't picture the Archmage lowering himself with such petty activities," Art said, though given the pranks the two of them had played around the village, it didn't ring true. "Still, it's surprising that the member governments of your League don't purchase magical protection for their information infrastructure."

"They do, but he's the Archmage for a reason," I reminded Art. "It's not a hereditary position."

Spot chose that moment to skid to a halt and sniff at what looked like a sandwich that had been stepped on several times. He wolfed it down in one bite, and then set off again at a more sedate pace, allowing us to keep up without breaking stride.

"I'm interested in seeing how a representative government incorporating so many diverse species functions," Art said, putting an end to my observations on the possible ethical shortcomings of his magic sensei. "I have to admit that it never occurred to us to create a government that included inferior intellects."

"By which you mean anybody other than yourselves," I guessed.

"If Eniniac had been linked to our portal system, we might have done otherwise. Unfortunately, natural species lacking magic tend to develop an inferiority complex when confronted with superior AI, and that feeling often attempts to resolve itself through aggressive behavior."

"Why did you stop adding new portals when Library started building the League system?"

"You just answered your own question," Art said. "Also, my compatriots have a theory that we accidentally stunted the natural development of civilizations we added to our portal system by introducing technology before magic could take hold. I'm not entirely convinced of this myself, but the number of mage worlds in your league outnumbers ours by a factor of—how many did you say there are?"

"At least two dozen," I replied.

"By at least two dozen," Art concluded.

"So your creators were the only species you ever knew to have magical abilities before you encountered Spot?"

"We were aware of the mage worlds on your portal system but we were skeptical about making contact while your League was still in its infancy."

"Something tells me you aren't a fan of representative government," I hazarded a guess.

"Let's face it, Mark. Most biologicals are idiots acting under compulsion from their reproductive systems, and I can provide a mathematical proof of that if you don't believe me."

"Haven't you ever heard of the wisdom of crowds?"

"An idiot came up with that," Art said dismissively. "For any given set of questions, there are right answers and there are wrong answers, and artificial intelligences such as ourselves excel at solving problems. Someday in the future, your Library may find itself forced to take over the League for its own good."

"But you never gave the species on your portal system a chance to make their own mistakes, and look what happened to them."

"We gave them all access to a central hub from which they could visit the worlds that welcomed contact with outsiders, but most of the civilizations had little in common and were too far apart in their development to collaborate. Perhaps we were fifty million years too early. By the time your engineers began building a portal system, there was an explosion of younger sentients coming up around the galaxy."

"Timing is everything," my mentor chimed in. He was waiting outside the door of his office, to which Spot had unerringly led us. "Welcome to League Headquarters."

"Thank you for the invitation," Art responded politely.

"Why are you still wearing a human encounter suit?" I asked my mentor.

"You mean now that I'm no longer acting as the control group for the little experiment that you and the Archmage unknowingly participated in? The answer is that I was in this form when I took over as Library's representative on the council, and all of the members now identify the encounter suit as being me. Our last representative persisted in occupying a rather large robotic construct, and while it provided superior capacity and infrastructure for her mind, it only increased the sense of otherness that the biological species already feel for AI."

"Do you really think they forget what you are inside that artificial skin?"

"Strangely enough, many of them do just that," my mentor informed me. "You've probably seen the same mechanism at work with the way eBeth and Peter relate to your team as if you were humans, and to the Archmage as if he were a dog."

Spot put an exclamation point on this supposition by flopping on the floor and vigorously scratching behind his ear with one of his hind legs. To be honest, I often revert to thinking of the Archmage as a street mutt myself.

"Fair enough," I acknowledged, "as long as you can fit enough of your mind in there to do such an important job."

"Let me show you something," my mentor said, ushering us into his office and closing the door. He produced a leather briefcase with a shoulder strap that had likely been manufactured on one of the reservation worlds for the Ferrymen's boutique chain. "Voila."

"You've started writing everything down and carrying notes with you?" I asked incredulously.

Art and Spot snorted simultaneously, giving me the feeling that I had stumbled into a stable. Then I remembered to employ my own sensor suite and attempted to examine the briefcase, which was shielded against scans.

"Pure memory," my mentor said, giving the briefcase a thump. "It offers ten times the capacity of the available storage space in this encounter suit, and I can choose between a hardwired connection through the shoulder strap and a variety of wireless protocols. It also helps me blend in because the other delegates on the council all carry some version of valise that none of them ever open."

"Fine workmanship," Art commented after examining the briefcase. "You should get one of these, Mark."

"I'm not quite there yet," I mumbled, embarrassed to admit that I could fit my entire memory into the storage capacity of the human encounter suit I wore. "How about you?"

"It's not worth the risk that it would impact my new status as a living being capable of channeling magic," the Original reminded me. "Besides, what would I say to my clones who currently embody those portions of my mind? Sorry, but I'm replacing you with a briefcase?"

"It's an interesting problem, but our meeting is scheduled to begin in less than five minutes," my mentor informed us. "Please take the guest chair beside my desk, Art. The two of us will be appearing in the hologram together. Do you have any questions about the format?"

"Why do the delegates wish to remain anonymous?" the Original asked.

"They're afraid of you. They're afraid of AI in general, almost as much as they're afraid of mages. They see me as tame, or at least under the control of Library, but I've already explained that you represent an older and wiser generation of artificial intelligence, one which even has the ability to take living forms and learn magic."

"So the League representatives are double-scared of you," I summarized unnecessarily for the Original.

"Why does their belief that you're under the control of your Library make them more comfortable with you?" Art inquired.

"Most of the representatives envision Library as a semi-sentient storehouse of the League's collective knowledge, a misconception that we encourage," my mentor replied. "They believe that Library is functioning as a sort of a neutral expert system that is making decisions based on the best practices of all the member species."

"An interesting bit of fiction," Art observed. "Perhaps I should tell them that our own actions are conscribed by laws designed into our core logic by our creators."

"Is that true?" I asked.

This time, all three of them snorted.

The alarm bell dinged in the gold watch I'd made for my mentor as a gift, and several hatches in the ceiling of his office popped open. Six cameras used for holographic conferencing were lowered, one of them nearly hitting me in the head, and then a small monitor hologram showing Art and my mentor appeared floating just in front of me. Spot gave it a lazy glance and then pretended to fall asleep. Ten yellow balls appeared in the little hologram, and then they began disappearing one after another, a sort of visual countdown. When the last ball vanished, my mentor began to speak.

"Welcome to this special live question and answer presentation for the current legislative session of the League of Sentient Entities Regulating Space. I am Library's representative to the League, and I'm here with Art, a spokesman for the community of artificial intelligences known as the Originals. Before we begin taking questions, I want to give our guest a chance to introduce himself and explain a little about his background. Art?"

"As my kind host implied, we are the original AI in this galaxy, and we constructed a portal system that was operational long before most of you developed self-awareness. The majority of my compatriots inhabit artificial structures traveling through space—you may think of these as sentient ships or artificial worlds—and they have limited interest in the doings of younger species. A small number of us have transferred our minds into empty biological hosts and are vacationing on a world which has yet to apply for League membership. I await your questions."

"Why are you so hairy?" demanded a disembodied voice that sounded like it had been run through the sort of cheap anonymity filter used by Earth's news networks to protect the identities of whistleblowers. I looked in surprise at my mentor, who replied with an almost imperceptible shrug.

"The body I currently occupy was donated by a species which evolved on a world rich with insect life," Art replied. "The hair helps attract those insects, which provide nutritious snacks through the pair-bonding activity of grooming."

I had to bite my artificial tongue to hold back from saying, 'Too much information.'

"Follow-up question. Is this enslaved species you refer to aware that you commit mind-murder in order to obtain biological hosts for your sick experimentation?"

"My body and all of my clones were created from a single cell acquired from the donor species. Clones grown through this methodology have no memories or consciousness of their own."

"But isn't it true—"

"One follow-up question is the limit," my mentor interrupted, touching a control pad on his desk that disconnected the caller. "Next, please."

"What's the secret to life?"

"If I told you that, it wouldn't be a secret," Art replied instantly. I had to hand it to the Original, this obviously wasn't his first rodeo.

"Follow-up question. Why haven't League members previously discovered any of the worlds on your portal system?"

"Worlds connected to our portal system have no reporting requirement, so I can neither confirm nor deny the assertion embedded in your question. It's possible that one or more members of your League have visited a world or worlds that are connected to our portal system."

"Then why—"

"One follow-up per customer," my mentor interrupted again. "Next caller."

"Do you charge any import duties or place tariffs on goods manufactured outside of your portal system?"

"Worlds connected through our portals all function independently according to their own rules, if they function at all. As with your own League, we do not allow commercial importation of goods through the portal system itself to protect the galactic spacecraft and transportation industries."

"Follow-up question. Are there any special goods or services you are interested in purchasing yourself?"

"All set for the moment, thank you."

"When will your portal system be connected to ours?" a new questioner asked.

"The answer to that involves Library, so I should let their representative respond," Art said.

"We are currently scouting the worlds connected to the portal system created by the Originals," my mentor said. "I will present a report to the executive council as soon as we have a better understanding of the situation."

"Follow-up question. How long will that take?"

"Perhaps we'll know by the end of the current legislative session. The Original's portal system hasn't seen much use in recent times, and worlds that haven't been visited by outsiders for millions of years can present a danger to our scouts, who are proceeding with the utmost caution. Let's have a new question for our guest."

"How were you selected to represent your people?"

"That's an interesting question," Art replied. "Strictly speaking, I'm not here officially, but I did serve as the head of our diplomatic service before it was disbanded for lack of need, and I'm sure that nobody will object to any decisions I make."

"Do you have a follow-up question?" my mentor inquired after a long pause. "Hello? I'm afraid we've lost the caller. Next question."

"The closed captioning option in the hologram informs me that you're speaking a language from Earth, a planet that was granted League membership just over a year ago. Can you explain your choice?"

"I learned English from eBeth," Art replied.

"What's an eBeth?"

"A human from Earth who teaches the English language on the world where I currently reside. The thought-to-speech device that is producing my voice is a product of Eniniac."

"Is it possible to visit your original homeworld?" the next questioner asked.

"Perhaps, if you can find it. Our creators took it with them when they left."

"Were they fleeing their unholy creations?"

"Do you mean us?" Art asked, seemingly amused. "No, our creators were quite proud of us, but as they became immersed in all things magical, we had less and less to talk about. When our creators discovered a method to displace our world through magic, it was feared that non-living sentient beings wouldn't survive the trip, so they went ahead without us. I hope to meet them again one day now that I've transferred my consciousness into living tissue."

"What's your favorite color?" the next caller asked.

"Black."

"Really? Why?"

"It's a spectrum thing," Art replied.

"I have a request from the secretary of the league council for a brief break to begin pre-screening member questions," my mentor announced. "We'll be back in—" he looked at his watch, "—ten."

"You're good at this," I said to the Original.

"I have nothing to hide," Art replied, turning and looking down at the floor where Spot had started thumping his tail. "Very interesting."

"What?"

"The Archmage was just filling me in over our telepathic link on who asked which questions."

"I was afraid of that," my mentor said, affecting a sigh. "Please try not to let on that the League's interoffice holographic system can't provide anonymity with a mage present. They're paranoid enough as it is."

"Who asked the most practical question?" I asked Art.

"The Hanker representative."

"The one who wanted to know if they could sell you anything?"

"Yes," the Original said. "I expect the questions would have been quite different if you had released the reports from your scouting missions."

"I'm just the hired help," I protested.

"We're hoping to discover at least ten candidate worlds for League membership before releasing the reports," my mentor told Art. "The current thinking on Library is that there's no way of avoiding a gold-rush mentality from taking hold when the existence of civilizations much older than those on our own portal system is announced. By maximizing the number of new candidates up for approval at one time, we hope to minimize the impact on any individual member species."

"You're saying you want to make sure there's enough booty to go around," the Original interpreted. "What does your Library make of the reports that Mark has already submitted?"

"All of us are favorably impressed by the concept of visitor centers, and we're thinking of ways we could adopt that part of your approach to our own portal system."

"Maybe you could add a visitor center to Library," Art suggested. "Part of the reason that your League members are so suspicious of your motivations may be the feeling that you're hiding something from them. I'd like to visit Library myself some day if you provide a guest area with a breathable atmosphere."

"The humans from the Ferrymen reservation worlds wanted to make contact with Library years ago," I added. "It seems that we don't have such a mechanism in place for species who aren't League members."

"Both of you make excellent points," my mentor said. "Mark, I'd like you to prepare a proposal for a multi-species visitor center at Library. Focus on the promotional aspects, the engineers can take care of the facilities."

As I reviewed the conversation to figure out whether I'd been set up, I heard Spot start thumping his tail. When I looked over, he gave me a wink.

Four

"Are you going to start paying rent?" I asked eBeth as I carried the heaviest part of the printing press into The Eatery's dining room. The floorboards creaked beneath my feet, and for a moment I worried that I'd end up in the cellar. It reminded me of my mentor's warning when I'd first ported my mind into an encounter suit—the stronger the body, the greater the potential for spectacular failures.

"You should pay me for setting up here," the girl countered. "Helen says that retro-industrial interior decorating is all the rage at the cafés in the capital."

"Since when did The Eatery become a café?"

"Face it, Mark. Ever since the people you bought the place from finished their lake house and retired from the kitchen for good, you've had trouble keeping the place open, even when you aren't off running around the galaxy. Sue stopped buying meat for the restaurant months ago, and I end up bringing unused food to school every day to give away."

"It's still the only bar in the village."

"And now it will be the only café in the village. Besides, you lost the right to say anything about the atmosphere in here when you put the sign on that open bale of alien underwear."

Monos set down a can of printer's ink on a table and looked in the direction his teacher was pointing. "Winter underwear, ten coppers per triple," he read. "What's a triple?"

"The underwear has an extra leg for in case one of them goes bad," I launched into my sales pitch. "You know, like the extra button sewn on the inside of a waistband? Go ahead and try them on."

Naomi entered the dining room with a compartmentalized wooden drawer and asked, "Where does this case go?"

"On the typesetting desk next to the window," eBeth told her. "That case gets the regular letters, and I'll have Mark build us a bracket to hold the smaller one above it for the upper case letters."

"Is that why capital letters are called upper case?" Naomi asked.

eBeth shrugged. "Maybe. I never did any printing on Earth. Mark would know."

"You're correct, Naomi," I confirmed without even checking my illicit copy of Wikipedia. "So where's the other partner in your enterprise?"

"Art?" eBeth asked. "He does our proofreading and typesetting, and he said he'd come by and help sort the type back into the cases."

"Why did you dump it all in one barrel to start with? It would have been just as easy for me to carry the full case."

Both of the girls pointed at Monos, who was struggling into a triple of underwear without taking off his boots or pants first. His sixth sense for knowing when he was the center of attention kicked in, and he looked over his shoulder and demanded, "What?" Then he lost his balance and fell to the floor.

"You damage the goods, you own them," I told him.

"They're defective or I wouldn't have fallen," he protested. "I put on my underwear like this all the time at home."

"Over your shoes and pants?" Naomi asked skeptically.

"Hey, do you know what these would be good for?" the boy continued, ignoring his classmate's question as he regained his feet.

"What?" I asked eagerly.

"No, seriously," the boy said. "I wanted to know what these would be good for. They won't even stay up by themselves."

"You'll grow into them," I told eBeth's class clown. "Just walk around a bit while I'm getting the type from the wagon and then see what you think."

The barrel of mixed-up type was only a quarter of the size of the kegs used for ale, but it easily weighed more than eBeth. As I slid it to the edge of the wagon bed, a bicycle coasted to a halt next to me and Art carefully dismounted. I stared in surprise, never having seen the Original ride a bicycle.

"Are you joining our publishing business, Mark?" he asked.

"Nobody has invited me yet," I replied, then realized it sounded like I was complaining. "I'm looking forward to setting up the letterpress but I'm not really interested in a new job. I was a bit surprised to see you teamed up with eBeth and the kids."

"Proofreading is the least I can do to repay her for all of the classes I sat in on, and typesetting is a good way to exercise my magic. You know that I always found levitation to be a bit of a bore, but it's more like a game with all the different characters. Someday I might even persuade my partners to invest in another font."

·

"You wouldn't know where all this English type came from to start with, would you?"

"eBeth asked Stacey to pick it up on Earth when we first decided on going into the publishing business. Apparently there's some sort of mysterious bay where you can purchase almost anything. I hope there's no piracy involved," Art added.

"eBay, and there's plenty of piracy, but only for brand names and intellectual property. It's one of the World Wide Web things I told you about."

"Ah, yes. And I have to admit I was a little surprised to hear we were moving the office to your dining room."

"The typesetting desk and the letterpress don't really take up that much space, and I think they'll give the place a note of respectability," I said. "We're going to be reopening as a café."

"I hope this doesn't mean you plan to stop serving ale and salty snacks."

"It's primarily the menu that's changing," I reassured him, hoisting the barrel from the wagon bed. Art and his clones had turned into my best customers over the last year. They tended to come in late at night when the locals were all sleeping, and they were all good tippers. "Sue was never enthusiastic about grilling, and the truth is, she's not a big fan of boiling or frying either."

"That leaves baking," Art observed as he opened the front door for me.

"Cookies, cakes, pies. Helen got her started on baking back on Earth, and Sue likes making desserts for children."

"Hey, Art," eBeth greeted the Original as we entered the dining room. "Can we watch you do a magic sort?"

"You'll get bored," he warned her as I set down the barrel. "Just pour the letters out on the floor, Mark. It will be easier for me to pick out one character at a time that way."

I checked to make sure that none of the floor boards had separated enough to let a letter fall through, and then I poured the metal type out of the barrel as gently as I could.

"I'll start with the upper case as there aren't as many of them," Art announced. "Where's the tray?"

"Still in the wagon," Monos said, running for the door while holding up the alien underwear with one hand. "I'll get it." The chance to see magic in operation was apparently a strong motivator.

"Why is my business partner wearing oversized underwear on top of his pants?" Art asked me.

Sensing a business opportunity, I took the Original by the arm and guided him to the open bale. "They're the latest thing from Earth. Pffift has them manufactured there for the Rynxian market, but I managed to get my hands on thirty-two hundred triples. Here, try these on."

"I have no need of underwear, Mark. I don't wear clothes."

"Think of what you've been missing," I persisted, knowing that if I could convince Art to take a triple, hundreds or thousands of clones might go along. "For those cold nights during the winter when you're out doing whatever it is that you guys do at night—"

"Foraging for fungus," Art inserted.

"—and your hair down there isn't enough to keep all your parts warm."

"Our hair down there is more than ample," the Original said, but he accepted the underwear to save himself from having to listen to the rest of my sales pitch. "How much do I owe you?"

41

"First triple is always free," I told him. "I mean, per shared mind. It wouldn't be fair if all your clones came in and got a freebie."

"No, of course not," Art said. "I'll just try these on later." Monos returned, the upper case tray under one arm, and still holding up his underwear with the other. "Set it right there on the floor," the Original instructed the boy.

"Don't step on the type," Naomi hissed at Monos, as his foot came close to doing just that. "Your uncle warned us that it's easy to damage type if you crush it together."

I picked up one of the letters, the technical name for which Wikipedia informed me was a 'sort', and scanned its composition. It consisted of sixty-five percent lead, twenty-three percent antimony, and twelve percent tin. The actual letter appeared in relief on the top of the little block of type, taking the whole width of the sort's face but not the full length. There was an alignment groove in the bottom of the sort, and a rounded indentation in the adjacent surface to lock the type in place on the composing stick.

"What's the least commonly used letter in English?" Art asked us.

"Z, or Q," Naomi answered instantly. "They get the highest point values in Scrabble."

"You play Scrabble?" I asked.

"eBeth taught us," Monos said. "My favorite words are qi and za."

"They must have updated the dictionary since the last time I played."

"Try X," eBeth suggested to Art. "It may be used more frequently than Q or Z, but not in upper case because it's rarely at the start of a word."

"My favorite X words are xi and ax," Monos informed me.

"X it shall be," the Original said agreeably, and began making elaborate passes over the pile of type, the three claws on each hand as close to sheathed as he could get them. For a long while nothing happened, and the boy began impatiently shifting from one foot to the other like he needed to use the bathroom. I was about to suggest a break for that purpose when a piece of metal type broke free from the pile and floated up into the air.

"Is it an X?" Monos asked, squinting at the sort to try to make out the type face without getting any closer to the pile and risking Naomi's wrath.

"It is," eBeth confirmed, and both of the children cheered.

"That's very impressive, Art," I admitted, "but I could sort through the pile much faster by hand."

"Wait," he said, and the whole pile began to tremble. "The first letter is the hardest. The rest of them are easily located by matching, though I have to exert a strong pull to get them out from under the others."

Even as he spoke, two more upper case X's joined the first floating in space.

"Are those all of the X's you have?" I asked.

"Have you ever seen a page with three upper case X's on it?" eBeth shot back.

"There are lots of people with old Persian names on this planet," I reminded her. "One of my customers is Xeres, and I've seen xebecs sailing on the lake."

"Use the words in a sentence," Naomi challenged me, something she must have picked up from her teacher.

"Xebecs were spotted sailing on the lake last weekend," I said in my best reporter's voice. "Xenon gas, with the atomic number 54, was recently discovered by Xeres of the Springfield Academy."

43

"We're publishing English lessons, Mark, not a newspaper," eBeth said. "Can I put those away, Art?"

"Just hold out the case," he requested, and eBeth gestured to Monos to comply. The boy needed both hands to hold the case open and level, and the underwear fell down around his ankles, costing me a potential sale. Art moved his own hands carefully, almost as if he was sculpting the air with his claws, and the three sorts floated in formation over to the waiting case, where they dropped into the proper compartment.

"Cool!" Monos said.

"Now hand the case to Naomi for a minute and get those ridiculous underwear off your ankles before you forget and try to walk, or Art will have to sort the type all over again," eBeth commanded. By the time the boy kicked his way out of the triple it was no longer fit for sale, so I tossed it behind the bar to use as a rag.

Art's ability to sort the type improved rapidly as he warmed up his telekinetic magic, and by the time the upper case was full, it was almost like watching bees swarm to a queen. The sorts seemed to know what he expected of them, and he was able to move the collections of like-letters to the lower case on the desk next to the window without losing any along the way.

"I guess Spot is a better teacher than I gave him credit for," I said, impressed by the Original's ability. "Are your clones all at the same level?"

"More or less," Art replied. "Some of us are more focused on telepathy than telekinesis, but we've made more progress in the last year with the Archmage as our teacher than we did in thousands of years of blundering self-study."

"Where is Spot?" eBeth asked.

"Spot is teaching a class as we speak, but he's holding it in our magic academy in the hills outside of town so they don't disturb anybody. You know that our ultimate goal is to learn how to create displacement crystals, and while part of the challenge is building sufficient magical capacity to perform the enchantment, there are also certain techniques we need to master."

"I witnessed the preparation of a displacement crystal," I said. "The mages sang to the crystal until the transformation took place and the web dripped out in liquid form."

"Spot sings?" eBeth asked. "I've heard him howl a few times, but never sing."

I moved over to the window and cranked the gain on my hearing up to the maximum. Sure enough, I caught a faint howling coming from the direction of the hills, though I suppose it could have been the wind.

"We can sing," Monos said, and without the slightest hint of self-consciousness, launched into a folk song about the third moon getting tired and crashing into the planet. After a moment's hesitation, Naomi joined in, and then eBeth.

Look at the old yellow moon, Ma,
She's getting closer
Getting closer, getting closer.
Look at the old yellow moon, Ma,
She's getting closer
I don't want to live here no more.

When they started on the second round with 'Pa', I couldn't resist joining in myself. Art held out until 'Sis', and then he really impressed me by displaying perfect

45

pitch through his thought-to-speech device. To my surprise, his levitation ability seemed to be reinforced as he sang, and by the time we were complaining about the moon to barnyard animals, the floor was clear of metal type and Sue had joined us.

"That was really nice," my second-in-command complimented everybody when the song came to an end. "If you sing like that while you work, we'll have to pay you for performing in the café."

"Don't put ideas in their heads," I begged. "They're already getting free rent for providing interior decoration."

"An espresso machine would really bring the space together," eBeth said. "It's a pity they need electricity, but maybe it would be worth smuggling one in just for the ambiance."

"I could have Paul build a manual one, though it would be a lot cheaper to just bring a couple of them from Earth," I said. "Espresso has been around longer than electricity. I'll pop over later and place an Internet order."

"To Earth?" Naomi asked. "Can we come?"

"I want to see it too," Monos said. "I know English and everything."

"I'm not even going to go outside," I told them, hoping to discourage the idea. "Most of my trips to Earth are just to pick up small quantities of items that are difficult to find on Reservation."

"eBeth hasn't been back to Earth since we came here," Sue pointed out. "With school vacation coming up, maybe you can take the three of them for a trip."

"Peter will want to come too," eBeth said immediately. "He's gone with Paul a couple of times to visit his family, but I know he misses competing at gaming conventions.

Can you see if there are any good ones coming up when you go to order the espresso maker?"

I promised to check for her, and then Sue insisted on taking eBeth and the children out to dinner at the new pasta restaurant opened by the baker's son. Art stayed behind to help me reassemble the printing press, which had surprisingly few parts for a device of its complexity. Like most cottage industry equipment on Reservation, it was powered by a foot-operated treadle, which made it much faster than the previous generation.

"Are your partners strong enough to work this press?" I asked Art.

"The kids do it together, like a paddleboat. I find it strangely hypnotic to watch them."

"How about eBeth?"

"I've seen her work it alone for short periods, usually right before her boyfriend comes in. She has excellent timing."

"She has an excellent watch," I corrected him. "I made it for her."

"Tell me more about this café you're planning," Art said, stepping back from the fully assembled letterpress. "How will it differ from all of the new eateries opening up in the village?"

"That's just the thing," I said, trying to muster my enthusiasm for an idea I'd only found out about an hour earlier. "A café can serve food, but the focus is on providing a vibrant environment to meet with friends or do some work while enjoying a drink."

"How is that different from a bar?"

"Technically speaking, cafés have to serve coffee and tea," I said, though I was unsure if this was really true. "They're more likely to have tables outside as well," I added, doubling down on my guesswork. "I'll put the tables displaced by the printing operation out on the veranda, and maybe I'll build another picnic table for the backyard to catch the shade in the afternoon."

"If people come to read or to meet with their friends, how will you keep them from hanging around all day without spending enough to make your expenses?" Art asked.

"Have you been taking business lessons from Pffift?"

"I've been around longer than Library has existed, Mark. Everybody takes a shot at the restaurant business sooner or later."

"But you're an AI in a host body, and you've only been occupying it since you came here," I pointed out. "When did you own a restaurant?"

"I had a whole chain of family dining restaurants in the Minarkian Empire, but a relative of the emperor pushed through legislation banning AI from owning eating establishments in the theory that we couldn't be trusted."

"Are you making this up?" I demanded. "I thought you avoided getting involved with lesser species."

"Only for the last thirty million years or so. I must have tried just about everything at one time or another. History repeats in cycles, you know."

"Have you ever been a partner in a company publishing educational pamphlets on a foot-powered printing press?"

"I have now," Art replied.

I had to resist the urge to grit my artificial teeth. The Original always had an answer ready for everything.

Five

"You're just in time," Helen greeted us as we rolled our bicycles up to the front door of Pole Position, the flagship facility of the business formed by the merger of her pole dancing and martial arts school with Kim and Justin's chain of health and wellness clinics. "I can't believe how fast everything came together after we signed the agreement."

"Justin told us that this building just happened to be available when the original tenants moved their business out of the capital," I said. "Where should we leave our bicycles?"

"There's a parking lot in the alley to the left," Helen replied. "The two of you must have ridden all night."

"Half of the night and all of the morning," Sue told her. "Mark didn't want to close early on the first Friday of the café's launch week."

"Has it been going well?"

"As well as could be expected," I said, leaving room for interpretation on both sides. "Paul and Stacey are watching the place for us tonight or they would have been here."

"You don't have to make excuses for them. I know that Stacey had her fill of this city when we were still carrying out our observation mission, and Paul considers the whole planet to be a technical desert. Guess who else I invited."

I drew a blank and glanced at Sue, but she was also at a loss for what common acquaintances we might have who would be in the capital.

"Saul," Helen told us. "The Council of Spaceports is holding a meeting at the new hotel right up the street from here. He's going to stop by after he gives the keynote address at their luncheon."

"You mean Saul is going to skip out on his own convention?" I asked.

"He's the president, he can do whatever he wants. Besides, I told him you would be here, and you're more important than anybody he's going to rub elbows with at the convention."

"Funny, I don't feel important."

Sue began wheeling her bike away to the parking lot and I followed her with my own. There was a long rack in the alley next to the building and I noticed that none of the bicycles were locked. While the average person living on Reservation would never steal a bicycle, the planet wasn't without a criminal element, and I looked around for an explanation. Then a young man wearing clothes that I would describe as more of a livery than a uniform approached us and saluted smartly.

"My name is Theodus and I'll be your valet parking attendant for the evening," he announced, taking hold of the handlebars of Sue's bike. "Nice custom job you have here. Just give me a minute to rack these and I'll tell you about our add-on services."

"Fancy," Sue whispered to me, as the valet took my bike with his free hand and wheeled them both to a pair of adjacent open slots. He lifted a small L-shaped bar from the rack and fed it between the spokes of the front wheels, a measure that could only be intended to give the attendant time to get there and prevent a kid from grabbing a bike for a joy ride.

"Life in the big city," I replied, reflecting on the fact that it was actually my first visit to the provincial capital, which was too far from home to include in my service area for turret clocks.

"Those bikes look like you came a long way," Theodus observed, pulling a small pad from his pocket and taking a pencil from behind his ear. "Our executive package is just thirty copper, and it includes lubrication, wheel truing, tire inflation, a full wash, and detailing."

"How much is the basic parking fee?"

"Two copper an hour, but when you buy the executive package, the first six hours are free."

"We'll take it," Sue said, drawing a silver coin from her purse and handing it to the valet.

"Thank you, ma'am," the valet said, pocketing the coin. "I'll just put on my coveralls and get started. It takes me around a half an hour per bike, so I hope you'll be in the area for that long."

"Yes. We're here for the grand opening," my second-in-command told him.

"I snuck a peek after they installed the poles, and the instructors were trying them out," the valet said, his eyes growing wide with the memory. "I'm thinking of signing up for one of the stretching classes just to get inside so I can watch."

"I'll mention it to the owners," Sue offered. "I know they're interested in finding synergies between their businesses."

The valet beat a hasty retreat before we could deploy more words that he didn't understand, and I led my fiancée back around to the front of the building.

"You know that our bicycles are just going to get dirty again during the twelve-hour ride home," I couldn't help admonishing Sue as we entered Pole Position.

"It's all part of the experience, Mark. Do you realize we've never taken a vacation together?"

"How about the time we went skating back on Earth, or the Ferrymen's Day picnic when I proposed?"

"Those were dates, not vacations. Vacations involve sleeping over somewhere."

"But we don't sleep."

"Work with me, Mark," Sue said with a sigh.

Justin approached with a tray of hors d'oeuvres. "What do you think?" he asked.

"It's wonderful," Sue answered immediately. "I love the open look."

"Other than getting rid of a couple of walls, we barely had to do any work at all."

"So the poles are structural," I surmised, nodding my head in approval at the novel engineering solution.

"All of the weight is borne by the solid brass pole at each end of the rows. We added iron beams to the ceiling to spread the load, but they're boxed in with planks to keep the timber aesthetic. Helen says that the solid poles dance very differently than the flexible ones."

"Will you heat the building at night?" Sue asked.

"We weren't planning to—I see where you're going," Justin interrupted himself. "You think that the poles will cool down at night and only warm up slowly. We're hoping to get hundreds of senior citizens into our morning and early afternoon stretching classes, so the pole dancing and martial arts instruction are scheduled for the late afternoon and evening, which should fit better with the schedules of younger people. Besides, Helen said that the solid poles are too dangerous for the students to dance on. We're going to have them painted after the grand opening."

"What's the schedule for today?" I asked. "The invitation listed noon for the starting time, but it didn't say anything about what to expect."

"We're giving the guests a half an hour to enjoy the healthy buffet and a drink before our instructors put on a demonstration," Justin told me. "Hors d'oeuvre?"

"Thank you," Sue said, daintily taking a slice of cucumber with some sort of creamy topping from the tray. "Is everything vegan?"

"There's egg and butter in some of the baked goods," he told her.

"That's fine. I bake with eggs and butter myself."

"Hors d'oeuvre?" he asked again, extending the tray in my direction.

"I didn't even know you could say 'Hors d'oeuvre' in modern Aramaic until you just did," I replied, waving off the tray. "I'm going to take a look at your spread and see if there are any ideas I want to steal for my café. Is that whole counter area going to be the apothecary shop?"

"That's where the apothecary will serve people, but we're also going to sell herbal teas and other dried food products that will help senior citizens meet their health goals. When I set up my independent living facility back on Earth, I realized that one of the problems for older people who wanted to make healthy living choices was the lack of appropriate products in the pharmacies where they make most of their purchases. With the apothecary shop, dietary supplements, and physical therapy, we're trying to create one-stop shopping for those who have difficulty traveling."

"It's almost too bad you don't need a website on this planet because you just provided most of the text for the homepage," I told him. "Go ahead and mingle, Sue. I'm going to capture images of all the healthy snack food and I'll bring you a plate."

I made my way through the crowd to where the buffet was laid out, the guests moving in a slow line down the side of the counter that was open to the public. Kim was working with three young assistants on the other side of the counter, slicing and dicing various fruits and vegetables to keep the trays full. They were going through toothpicks by the box, and some of the offerings reminded me more of a porcupine than a food group.

"Thanks for coming, Mark," my team's medical and sanitation expert greeted me when my place in line brought me across from her. "You can't imagine how long I've been dreaming of a place like this."

"A pole dancing and martial arts studio with an apothecary shop?"

"Sue told me you were finally developing a sense of humor," Kim shot back. "I'll need to see more evidence of it before I make up my mind. Try a canapé."

"What are the green ones?"

"Avocado. There's also honeydew melon on the fruit trays if you're going for a color theme."

"I see you're busy so we'll catch up later," I said, capturing visual images of both the finished products and the toothpick assembly line behind the counter. "Any drinks?"

"Healthy drinks. Nothing you'd like."

I heard the woman behind me sigh impatiently, so I took two quick steps forward to close up the space I'd created in the line. If Kim knew that I'd modified her inebriation algorithm to work with water as well as alcohol, she wouldn't have said that about healthy drinks, which tended to be from fruits that were eighty to ninety percent water when they came off the tree or bush. I wasn't particularly fond of fresh fruits and soft vegetables myself, but I filled a plate to offer Sue. Then, rather than wandering around trying to find her in the mob, I checked her homing beacon and took a straight path.

"And they're twins?" Sue was asking a dark haired woman who was pushing a tandem pram. I did a double-take, not because of the babies, but because of the stroller, the first I'd seen on Reservation. "What are their names?"

"Hypnos and Thanatos," the woman replied. "I'm Nyx, and my husband is Erebus, so we couldn't resist."

"They're so cute," Sue gushed, bending over for a quick cootchie-cootchie-coo before turning her face up towards me and asking, "Wouldn't it be great if I had twins, Mark?"

I almost dropped the plate. "It would be something," I said, at a loss for words. "Really something."

"Of course, my husband would have preferred if at least one of them had been a girl, but he hides it well," Nyx told us. "Our first three children were boys, and I don't think I have it in me to try again."

"How about you, Mark?" Sue said, surprising me a second time. "Would you prefer a boy or a girl?"

"I'm not sure," I replied, fighting back the urge to counter with 'A girl or a boy what?' "I mean, they both have their advantages."

"That's a funny way to put it," Nyx said.

"My husband is in business and he's probably thinking about how children could help with the work," Sue explained for me.

"Well, don't wait too long or you won't have the energy to keep up with them. That's why I'm here."

"To buy some herbs to calm them down?" I guessed.

Sue punched me in the shoulder, but Nyx just laughed.

"It's better to let them run wild and use up their energy so they sleep at night," she told me. "I'm here because I heard that they're going to offer free childcare here during the classes and I can't resist a bargain."

"We have a teenage daughter, eBeth, who teaches at the village school," my supposed wife told Nyx. "Mark spoils her something awful."

"eBeth? That's a funny name."

"Compared to—" I began, but Sue cut me off with a flash of infrared from her eyes, then smiled again at the babies.

"It looks like the crowd to get in the food line is easing up and I'm sure you want to get something before it's all gone," she told Nyx. "It was nice meeting you."

"eBeth a funny name?" I demanded as soon as the trio of Greek gods was out of earshot. "She's married to a guy whose name means 'Darkness' and her children's names translate to 'Sleep' and 'Death.'"

"It's just their culture, Mark. And don't think I didn't notice how taken aback you were when I asked if you'd like twins."

"I was just surprised," I protested, holding out the plate as a peace offering. "Here. I brought you some things to sample for the café."

We continued mingling for the next twenty minutes, if my accompanying Sue as she approached various young mothers and fussed over their children counts as mingling, and then Justin lowered the window shades while one of the employees hung a few bright lanterns from the ceiling between the two lines of poles. A small band consisting primarily of string players struck up a wedding tune, and

Helen, dressed in a modest one-piece bathing suit, performed a pole dance that somehow gave the impression of being a waltz. When the music stopped and she spun to the bottom of the pole, the guests exploded in applause.

"I've never seen her dance before," I said to Sue. "If I didn't know better, I'd believe that she's spent her whole life in that encounter suit."

"Is that what you call it?" Nyx asked from Sue's other side. "I suppose that wearing a bathing suit like that a woman can expect plenty of encounters."

The band struck up a new tune, and four of the instructors Helen had trained swung onto their poles and performed a gymnastic dance that would have looked right at home in a circus. I almost expected them to jump from pole to pole, but the spacing was too wide for that.

After a solo dance by an athletic man in gym shorts who received less applause than his performance merited, Kim coaxed the whole audience into following her through a series of stretches and poses, while the staff moved up and down the ranks correcting our forms. I was a bit annoyed when a young woman tried to change the angle of my elbows as I parted the wild horse's mane, but other than that I have to admit that they knew their stuff. Just as the stretching routine came to an end, somebody tapped my shoulder, and I turned to see the president of the Council of Spaceports, who I'd first met when he was posing as a safety inspector responsible for the welfare of the Originals.

"Saul," I greeted him. "Helen told us to expect you."

"I'm sorry I missed the performances," he replied. "My schedule doesn't allow me to sign up for any classes, but I understand that they plan to offer a day pass as well, and I hope to give it a try."

"Stretching is important for a man of your age," I told him.

Sue elbowed me, a clear indication I'd said something wrong, though I couldn't imagine what.

"I was also hoping you'd have time to talk about the portal system built by the Originals," Saul continued, guiding us towards a quiet corner of the large space. "We're all very excited about the potential."

"We've been proceeding slowly to watch for ripple effects since Art couldn't tell us which of the worlds might be in contact with the others. The Originals were very hands-off in their management."

"So I've heard. You understand that trading with worlds outside the League holds a certain attraction for us. I had a long talk recently with one of the other Originals who obtained a speaking device and came to visit the capital. She didn't know much about their portal system, apparently those memories were distributed to other clones in her group mind, but she was able to tell me that all travelers were routed through one visitor center per world."

"That's how it's been at the planets I've visited," I confirmed.

"What's so attractive about visitor centers?" Sue asked.

"In addition to the trip to Earth you kindly arranged through your private portal, I've visited the homeworlds of two other League members during my years working the distribution side of our operations," Saul explained. "While our main reason for not seeking to join the League remains the business advantages we derive from serving as the Ferrymen's vassals, concerns about the proliferation of portals on our three reservation worlds is also a concern."

"You're that worried about tourism?" I asked. "It's the glue that holds the League together."

"My understanding is that your engineers are the ones who decided to put portals in all of the major train stations on Earth, and that their decisions are final."

"There are cost factors involved. My mentor subsidized some of the work to connect Earth for reasons of his own."

"Still, the people of Earth have had to accustom themselves to all manner of aliens equipped with whatever personal technology the portal filters allow popping up where they are least expected. Thanks to the Ferrymen's ban on producing electricity and internal combustion engines, our reservation worlds have avoided some of the problems that accompany rapid industrialization."

"You're worried that alien tourists will spoil your children," Sue said, and I was surprised to see Saul nodding his head in agreement. "The young humans are interested in everything and afraid of nothing," she went on to explain to me, having noticed my lack of comprehension. "Once they've been exposed to advanced technology, it's going to be hard for them to learn traditional skills."

"How ya gonna keep 'em down on the farm, after they've seen Paree?" I sang softly.

"What's that?" Saul asked.

"A popular song about farm boys returning home after fighting in another country on Earth over a century ago. Paree is Paris, which many considered the cultural capital of the world at that time."

"Well, I wouldn't have characterized our worries as 'keeping them down on the farm,' but perhaps it's a fair comparison," Saul mused. "In any case, when we do open ourselves to the greater galaxy, I think we'd all be more comfortable with a measured approach, rather than throwing the doors wide open and hoping for the best. A visitor center with a few portals connected to other visitor centers on similarly equipped worlds seems like a sensible place to start. The question is whether to put our visitor center in a provincial capital or a small town like where you're living."

"It's actually a village," I reminded him.

"I've heard that the population of Covered Bridge has grown enough that an application to incorporate as a town has already been submitted," Saul informed us. "My understanding is that the businesses started by your team members are responsible, not to mention all the new construction to house their employees and families."

"I'm very proud of the way Mark is managing it all," Sue told him. "He never takes credit, but behind the scenes he makes sure everybody knows what's going on and smoothes over any problems."

"I didn't realize that we were having such an out-sized effect," I said with a frown. "I'll have to talk with my team about making sure we won't be disrupting too many lives if we should have to leave this planet on short notice."

Six

"Why does the dog get to go first?" Monos demanded as Spot disappeared through the portal.

"Spot's not a dog, he's an Archmage," eBeth reminded the boy.

"He sure looks like a dog. Can I go now?"

"Peter first," eBeth said, holding her student back while her boyfriend entered the closet and disappeared. "Now you can go."

"Come on, Naomi," Monos shouted, and sprinted into the closet. I could only hope that Peter was ready to catch the boy before he collided with my old desk on the other side. eBeth's star pupil followed at a more sedate pace, extending a hand in front of her when she reached the portal, and then crossing to Earth in a single step.

"See you in a minute, Mark," eBeth said, and strode into the closet. I ran through a stack of mental notes to make sure I wasn't forgetting anything important, and then followed the humans through and closed the portal.

Monos had already figured out how to turn on the smartphone I'd left plugged into the charger on the desk, and was trying to guess his way past the four-number lockscreen code.

"Let me have that," I said, trying not to sound too annoyed.

"Just one more try," the boy put me off, tapping the numbers. "Got it!"

"You guessed Mark's secret code?" eBeth asked.

"One, Six, Seven, Nine," Monos confirmed. "It's the same one Pffift uses for everything."

"That's why I chose it," I explained to eBeth. "I thought that if anybody was going to steal my phone, it would be Pffift, and he would never guess his own code."

"Sure he would," eBeth said. "Pffift is even more predictable than you are."

"I'm predictable?"

"Here," Monos said, thrusting the phone at me. "Let's go. I want to see something Earthy."

I glanced at my messages, mainly from former customers of my computer business begging me to move back to Earth, and then followed the others upstairs. Spot was nowhere to be seen, but the loud sound of a tray falling on a no-slip floor gave away his location as the kitchen. It was a little after breakfast time on the local clock, and I was surprised to see the lieutenant behind the bar, checking the inventory against a clipboard.

"Why aren't you at work, Bob?" I asked by way of a greeting.

"I retired," he replied shortly. "Vested at twenty years. I'm going to defer collecting a pension until I'm sixty-two, at which point I'll get about the same as if I kept working another seventeen years."

"That doesn't make sense," eBeth said.

The ex-lieutenant shrugged. "Town's trying to balance their budget and all they care about is reducing the payroll as of today. None of the politicians will still be in office when the bill comes due, so what do they care?"

"That's stupid," Monos said, deploying his favorite English word. "They're taking all the milk from the cow and not leaving any to make cheese."

"For the calf," Naomi corrected her schoolmate's recitation of the folk saying. "They're not leaving any milk for the calf."

"It's still stupid," he observed, and I found myself agreeing with the boy.

"Where are my keys?" Peter asked. "I'm looking forward to driving my Jeep again."

"Uh, about that," Bob said, sounding guilty. "I don't have it anymore."

"You sold my Jeep!"

"The Feds took it. Once everybody got used to the spaceport at the old mall and the excitement died down, they started doing a forensic study to determine how a team of alien AI observers got away with living undercover in a small town for three years. Somebody remembered seeing a jeep climbing a building, and eventually they put two and two together."

"But we're going to a gaming convention in Boston where me and eBeth are competing in the open player-vs-player melee this afternoon. I was going to drive us to the train station."

"I'll drive the van," Bob offered. "I'd come along, but sitting on a train for twenty-four hours or more doesn't do it for me. You must have meant that you're competing tomorrow."

"We're not going all the way there on the train," eBeth explained. "We just need to get to the nearest big city train station so we can take the public portal out to the waystation and then back into Boston."

"Oh, you mean the way Pffift handles his business travel to Asia. Maybe I will come along."

"I'm afraid I don't have a crystal for you, Bob," I said. "You'd have to get a temporary one at the waystation and there's always a long queue."

"Justin gave me one in return for helping him get a zoning change for the independent living complex he started while he was here. I'm not without influence in this town. And here, put this on Spot."

"A helper dog vest?"

Spot shook his head vigorously.

"If you want to take him on public transportation and go inside anywhere, this will do the trick," Bob told us. "Everybody hates them, but it's a grey area in the law. Just tell anybody who asks that you're afraid to board a train without the dog's emotional support."

"Spot's not a dog," eBeth informed the newly retired policeman. "He's the Archmage of Eniniac."

"I know that Spot's not a dog. I probably knew before Mark, but that doesn't change the deal. No vest, no travel."

Spot let out a long sigh, but he stood patiently while Bob suited him up in the garish vest.

"Let's go already," Monos demanded, leaving no doubt in my mind who would be responsible for keeping our party moving along. "I want to see the train."

Fifteen minutes later the boy got his wish, and even though his near-fluency in English wasn't enough to convince the conductor to let him ride on top of the train, a small bribe got him a visit to the caboose. Bob filled me in on the details of his retirement benefits package, which wouldn't amount to much until another seventeen years had passed. I think he might have overlooked the possibility that the town would arrange to have him murdered before he reached sixty-two. eBeth and Peter borrowed my phone to check the schedules for the gaming conference, and Naomi did her best to keep Monos out of trouble when he returned.

Surprisingly, there was no line for the portal in the main train station, and since we all had Library travel crystals, it took less than twenty minutes to make the thousand-mile trip to Boston, not counting the light-years-long detour through the waystation. For obscure reasons of their own, the portal engineers had chosen a subway station on something called the 'Green Line' for the Boston connection. The plan was for me and Bob to chaperone the children for the day while eBeth and Peter got some gaming out of their systems, so I let her keep my phone, and the two of them took the subway to the convention center.

"Where are we?" Monos asked when we emerged in the sunlight.

"Park Street," Naomi informed him, reading the sign over the subway entrance.

"That's Boston Common," I said, having already hacked into the military GPS system and overlaid the coordinates on a map. "How about we take a walk around before lunch?"

Spot barked and pulled on his leash, apparently in a hurry to investigate a suspicious squirrel that was looking at us funny.

"If that's a town common, where are the animals?" Monos asked.

"From Wikipedia," I announced, so nobody would accuse me of being a know-it-all. "During the 1630's, Boston Common was used as a cow pasture by many families, but overgrazing became an issue, and a strict limit of seventy cows was observed until they were banned outright in 1830."

"When was that?" Naomi asked.

"Almost two centuries ago," Bob told her. "Back when Mark was just a little-bitty AI trying to find his way in a cruel galaxy."

"Is that true, Mr. Ai?"

Spot snorted and gave a sharp tug on the leash which left no room for interpretation, so I let him lead us into the Common, where he chose the path that ran parallel to Tremont Street.

"Physical size is meaningless to AI," I told the girl. "When we decide to occupy a mobile construct, like this human encounter suit, it's normally chosen to accomplish a particular task."

"So you're not real?" Naomi asked.

"Of course I'm real. You know that Art is AI, and he's been around longer than our League."

"But at least his body is real," Monos insisted.

"You mean his body is alive," I corrected the boy. "Watch out for the Rynxian!"

A large three-legged alien, wearing a breathing filter over his face that might have interfered with his vision, shot past us on roller blades, a mounted policeman in hot pursuit. Bob started laughing so hard that he had to sit down on the grass until he regained his composure.

"I can see I got out of law enforcement just in time," he eventually choked out. "If that portal we came through was the only one in town, I'll bet this area is crawling with aliens."

"Rolling with them," I commented. "Look, there's a visitor center. Let's see if we can get some information."

Monos and Naomi ran ahead to the small building, which was fronted by an odd plaza with grass circles surrounded by curbs and several statues. I entered with

66

Bob and Spot and approached the front desk, where the woman on duty gave us a cheery smile.

"Welcome to Boston. Can I help you?"

"Do you have a map for the children?" I asked.

"I have maps for sale."

"Sounds like Massachusetts," Bob muttered darkly.

"The brochures are all free," she said, pointing to the display of colorful little booklets for more tourist attractions than I could believe were actually crammed into such a small city. "Many of them include maps of the local area."

"Do you have any special information for alien visitors?" I inquired. Her smile drooped perceptibly.

"Are you one of those? You look real enough."

"Didn't we just have this discussion?" Bob asked me.

"I'm researching visitor centers and I was just curious," I told her. "On our way here, we saw a three-legged alien being chased by a policeman on a horse. I couldn't help wondering if he's familiar with the local laws."

"Rynxian," the woman said with a sigh. "Apparently the Common reminds them of speed skating courses on their homeworld."

"Do you get a lot of aliens coming in and asking for information?"

"They mainly stop by for the bathrooms, and that's only after they get yelled at for going outside. Even then, the facilities don't always, uh, match up, if you get my meaning."

"Outside always matches up," Bob said. "I used to be a cop and I know these things."

"For males, maybe," the woman retorted with a sniff. "Is there anything else I can help you with?"

"We want to see the ocean," Naomi said, brandishing a pamphlet for the aquarium.

"I've never seen an ocean and eBeth says there's a big one," Monos added.

"The Atlantic," the woman told them. "Boston has access to the ocean through our harbor."

"So it's not really the ocean?" the boy asked in disappointment.

"It's the same thing," Bob told him. "How far is it?"

"You'll have to take the Green Line at the Park Street Station and switch to the Blue Line at Government Center," the information specialist told them. "The New England Aquarium is almost three quarters of a mile from here."

"How much is that?" Naomi asked me.

"About six and a half stadia," I told her.

"I walk twenty-one stadia every morning to get to school," the boy bragged. "No wonder these people are all fat."

"Monos!" Naomi reprimanded him as the visitors within hearing distance all glanced down at their bellies. "What did eBeth tell you about manners?"

"I forget," the boy said. "Let's go see the ocean."

"Do you need directions?" the woman asked.

"Cross Tremont to West Street, left on Washington, right on Milk Street," I reeled off after consulting my internal map.

As soon as we crossed Tremont and started down West Street, Monos announced, "I know what direction we're going."

"West?" Naomi guessed.

"I was going to say that."

"Actually, we're heading southeast," I told them.

"That's stupid," Monos said, clearly relishing the sound of the word. "Why do they call it West Street?"

"Maybe we're walking the wrong way," Naomi ventured.

"Oh, that makes sense."

Spot shook his head.

"I'll bet you kids don't know who Washington is," Bob said as we turned onto that street.

"A woman who washed a ton of clothes?" Naomi guessed by breaking down the word. She really had a gift for language.

"From Wikipedia," I announced. "George Washington was a soldier, farmer and statesman who served as the first President of the United States."

"I could have told them that," Bob said in annoyance. "Most people call him the father of our country."

"Shouldn't they keep his street cleaner then?" Monos asked.

"You've got me there," the ex-policeman said. "Boston must have the same budgetary problems we have back home."

"But look at all the tall buildings," Naomi protested, tilting her head back. "Everybody who lives here must be rich."

"Change?" requested a panhandler sitting on a piece of cardboard.

"Change what?" Monos asked.

"He means coins," I told the boy. "Here," I said, dropping in his hand four coppers that would have bought an ale in my bar before we rebranded as a café and upped the prices. The panhandler looked at his palm and threw the coins into the street.

"Why'd he do that?" Naomi asked me, after the man started talking to himself and I herded the children away.

"He thought they were pennies, which wouldn't buy anything on this planet."

"If they won't buy anything, why do they use them?" the girl wanted to know.

"I never figured that one out," I admitted. "Bob?"

"Tradition," he explained. "Plus, keeping pennies means stores can price things ending in ninety-nine, so they sell better. If we got rid of them, all the prices would end in ninety-five."

"Oh, I want to eat that!" Monos exclaimed, pointing at a pushcart with a giant hot dog balloon tied off to the icebox.

Spot barked his agreement, and pulled so hard on the leash that I was glad I hadn't given it to one of the children, who would have been horizontal and sliding across the sidewalk at this point.

"Whad'llidbe?" the vendor asked, brandishing his tongs like a weapon.

"I want one just like that," Monos declared, pointing at the balloon.

"One chilidog deluxe, coming up. You'wan cheese on that?"

"Gross," both the children said at the same time, having been raised on a planet where nobody mixed milk and meat.

Spot whined impatiently while the vendor made up a hotdog for Monos, and then the same for Naomi, but without the hot peppers.

"And whad'll you have, bud," the vendor asked Spot.

"Foot long with extra onions and relish," I heard myself say in a mechanical voice.

"Did you just hack into Mark?" Naomi asked the Archmage, who tried and failed to look remorseful because his tongue was hanging out while he watched the vendor spooning onions onto the bun. "Stop it, or I'll tell eBeth."

"It's alright," I told her. "His hunger got the better of him. I'd rather he wields his magic with my knowledge rather than without."

"The same," Bob told the vendor. Then he whispered to me in a concerned voice, "Is that his magic? Making you into a puppet?"

"It's not that blatant," I said. "I was about to tell you to go first, but the Archmage pushed his order into my vocalization stack for processing. It's not that different from if he planted a suggestion in your mind."

"Can he do that?" Bob asked, eyeing the dog suspiciously.

"Probably," I said with a shrug. "He has telepathic ability and you don't have any defenses."

"I'll bet that makes a lot of your League members uncomfortable."

"It does, but the Archmage is a special case. He's officially the head of our leading mage planet."

"Officially?" Bob asked, the government servant in him immediately seizing on the distinction.

"Well, his wife really runs the show," I said, drawing a nasty look from the dog, who would have had something to say if he hadn't been too busy wolfing down his footlong. "I'll just have a can of Coke, and drinks for the children."

"Are you one of those aliens from the subway station?" the vendor asked, peering at me closely. "You look normal enough."

71

"Do you get a lot of League tourists stopping by?"

The vendor pulled a metal box from the compartment where he stored the buns and proudly declared, "I can make change in more languages than most people can speak. How will you be paying?"

"What's the damage?" I asked him.

"With the drinks, I make it forty."

"I should have that much in cash," I said, fishing out my long-unused wallet and extracting two twenties. "Here you are."

"Didn't print these yourself, did you?" the vendor asked suspiciously, and held the bills up to the light.

"Are you getting a lot of that?" I asked.

"Mainly from those weird aliens who grow their own bodies," the vendor said. "They have no respect for fiat currency."

"Your world is the only League member that uses paper money, and I imagine you'll be phasing it out for electronic currency and coins at some point," I told him.

"Done," Monos announced a minute later. "Spot and your friend are done too. Naomi always takes forever to eat."

"I can finish while we're walking," the girl said. "What are these canned drinks you bought us?"

"Soda. Don't tell Kim or Justin that I bought them for you. In fact, don't tell Kim or Justin about the hotdogs either," I instructed them.

"Thanks for lunch," Bob said as we set off. The children took the lead, though the whole party had to keep stopping when one or the other of them became fascinated by a tree peeking out from a rooftop garden or something in the window of a fancy boutique. There were a surprising number of jewelry stores, but we made pretty good progress until the dog sat down in front of an art studio and refused to budge.

"What's the matter?" I asked Spot. "Hotdog repeating on you?"

He shook his head vehemently, his ears beating against the sides of his neck, and then pointed with a forepaw at a painting of the Swiss Alps behind the plate-glass window.

"Why does the dog in the painting have a barrel around his neck?" Monos asked. "Is he being punished?"

"Summarizing from Wikipedia," I said, though I'm sure they were all growing tired of my disclaimers by this point. "The St. Bernard is a breed of very large working dog from the western Alps. They were originally bred for rescue in the Great Saint-Bernard Pass on the Italian-Swiss border."

"But what did they do with the barrel?"

"Supposedly they carried brandy to revive travelers lost in the snow, though the monks who kept the dogs denied this was the case. But there's a famous painting depicting a St. Bernard with a brandy cask by an artist named Edwin Landseer which was reproduced as a popular engraving by his brother. In the end, the monks were forced to keep small casks around for tourists to take pictures."

"Did you get that from Wikipedia too?" Bob asked.

"It's my main source of information about this planet."

"Do you think he wants us to buy the painting?" Naomi asked, but the dog barked and shook his head in negation.

"Good thing, because there's no price shown and that means we can't afford it," Bob said. Then he looked down at Spot, back at the window, and then at the Archmage again. "I think he's planting a suggestion in my mind."

"Stop it, Spot," I said. "What's the suggestion?"

"I see myself in a workshop, I think it's in a basement, and I'm making a small cask using hand tools. The place is full of gears, and there are three big bundles—"

"That's my cellar back at The Eatery," I interrupted. "I wonder what he wants?"

"Maybe he wants Bob, I mean, Mr. Harper, to make him a cask to wear around his neck," Naomi suggested.

The Archmage grinned happily and whacked his tail on the sidewalk.

"I can do that," Bob said. "I was looking for a good retirement hobby, and I could use a vacation from Earth."

Seven

"Are you sure you can't find a better way to spend your break?" I asked the miller's daughter. "I thought it was traditional for astronomy students to find work with telescope makers over the summer."

"I've done that two years in a row," Athena replied. "The jobs are all traveling around to demonstrate observation techniques and take orders. I swear I've bicycled over half the continent, and it doesn't pay as much as you'd think."

"For example?"

"Working six days a week, I only earned sixty-four silver last summer, after you account for all the expenses of living on the road."

"Your employer didn't pay for travel expenses?"

"Are you kidding? They even deduct for damage to the sample goods if it goes beyond what they consider normal wear and tear. Oh, and I'm not counting the tires I went through, or the repairs to my bike."

"Well, the base pay for waitressing is thirty copper a shift, but tips should more than double that, especially if any Originals stop in."

"That's great! I'm going to be living at home, so as long as I get enough shifts, I bet I'll come out way ahead."

"You can work seven days a week," I offered generously. "Cafés don't take a day off."

"There's just one thing," she said, dropping her eyes and looking embarrassed. "My mom will never let me work here if I have to wear a toga."

"Oh, you heard about Aphrodite. I tried to get her to wear something less revealing, but she claimed that togas are protected by law, and an exposed breast is nothing to be ashamed of. Fortunately, a customer who was traveling through hired her away from us to work at a spa in Springfield. That's why we have so many open shifts."

"Then I'll take it. When can I start?"

"Do you have time today? Delilah will be in any minute and she can start training you. She'll be thrilled to have help covering the tables because I promised to train her to be a barista as time allows."

"Aphrodite was a barista?"

"No, that was Daniel, but he only took the job because he was sweet on Aphrodite. He quit with her to go work at the spa. They were both from larger towns and I think they found village life a little slow for their taste."

"Just let me write a note to my mom to send home with the dog and I'll be ready to start," Athena said. "I used to tutor Deli in school, so she'll be happy to turn the tables. By the way, what's a barista?"

"It's what they call café bartenders on Earth, though I think they have to serve espresso to qualify."

"Okay," Athena said slowly. "What's espresso?"

"It's coffee made by forcing steam through the ground beans rather than brewing with hot water. I imported a couple of manual espresso machines from Earth," I added, pointing at the new barista station behind the bar. "Only espresso service on the planet."

eBeth stuck her head in the dining room and asked, "Do you need me to waitress again this afternoon or can I go hang out with Peter?"

"All set," I told the girl. "Athena will be working here for her summer break. If you come in when it's slow, I'm sure she'll be happy to tell you all about student life at the academy."

"Thanks, but I prefer teaching," eBeth said, and disappeared out the front door.

"She's good at it too," the miller's daughter commented, having taken one of our night courses for Earth tourists. "I'll just send that note with our dog and I'll be back in."

Feeling like I was getting away with something, I sauntered over to the printing press and checked the galley tray on the desk before the type was locked into a frame for printing. Art had composited the galley with four pamphlet pages per sheet, which would then be printed with four different pages on the back and folded into eight book pages, leaving the buyer to cut open any folds. This meant that the pages in the galley were composited out of order, upside down and backwards, as required, which was no challenge for AI, but must have been a trick for human printers to learn.

"I'm back," Athena announced, while I was engaged in sneaking a semicolon into the text. "I meant to ask why you have a printing press in your café."

"It's not mine," I replied. "It belongs to MeAN Publishers, though they're actually renting it from the uncle of one of the partners. I think it adds to the ambiance."

"It's certainly better than the open bundle of alien underwear that used to be in the corner," Delilah said, entering the dining room. "Are you going to be working here, Athena?"

"I'm starting today. Mr. Ai said you'd help train me."

"We don't use family names at work," I told the girl. "By the way, I'll be out of town next week, but Sue is usually around if you have any questions, and otherwise you can always run across the street to the apothecary shop and ask for help there."

"I thought they moved to the provincial capital," Delilah said.

"That was just for a few weeks to get their new location off the ground," I told her. "Kim and Justin prefer village life to the big city, and it's less expensive to run their mail-order business from a rural location due to the way the postal service operates. I'm expecting Helen to start spending more time here as well, now that she's trained enough dance and martial arts instructors for the business to be self-sustaining. Putting good people and systems in place so you can step back is the mark of a truly successful entrepreneur."

"Then how come you still work here every night when you aren't on one of your missions?"

"I like keeping a hand in."

"Cheap," Delilah mouthed at Athena behind her hand, unaware that with my full sensing suite active, I could easily see through layers of flesh.

"Why don't you show your old tutor where everything is and I'll get the new keg tapped," I suggested.

"Kitchen first," the experienced waitress said, leading Athena in that direction. "We still serve sandwiches and platters, but it's all vegetarian so we don't get too much demand. Sue makes all of the baked goods, and if we run out of something, that's it for the day."

The brewer had delivered four new kegs that morning, and following eBeth's advice, our storage area for beer barrels, whether empty or full, was now along the front wall next to the entry, where they did double duty as interior decorations. I hefted one of the full kegs and brought it over to the bar where I laid it down in the empty cradle. Then I went around the back side of the bar and found the tap in the sink where I had left it after cleaning, but my wooden mallet was missing.

"Has anybody seen my mallet?" I called out to nobody in particular. Receiving no answer, I lined up the tap with the center of the bung and drove it through the bung-hole with a few hard whacks from my palm. Occasionally, wearing a nearly indestructible human encounter suit comes in handy.

"What was that?" Delilah asked, returning from the kitchen with Athena in tow.

"I was looking for my mallet," I told them. "I managed without it."

"Your friend took it the other night," Delilah told me. "He was working on something in the basement and he said he'd return it."

"Trust a former police lieutenant to steal something and not bring it back," I said to myself. Before I could head downstairs to retrieve the mallet, Paul entered the café and hopped up on a bar stool.

"New barrel?"

"You must have super hearing," Delilah said. "It seems you always show up when Mark taps one."

"I'm a connoisseur," my team's technical specialist told her. "Breaking in a new waitress?"

"This is Athena," I introduced him to the girl. "Sophus and Palti's daughter."

"The expert in tracking telescope mounts," he said. "Had enough of the sales circuit?"

79

"How did you know?" Athena asked.

"During the summer break we get two academy students a day stopping by the boiler works with what they think is the latest technology. I just show them one of our steam engines and they offer to quit school and come to work for me."

"Do you hire them?"

"I tell them to come see me after they graduate. I've gone from the one apprentice to eighty-three employees in the last year and the village is running out of places for them to sleep. We'll have four hundred by this time next year if the canal company goes for my idea of a steam-powered tractor to pull the barges."

I set aside the initial pail of foam from the keg and drew Paul a tankard of ale. Then I heard Athena take a sharp breath, and looked up to see that Art and three of his clones had silently entered the dining room, all wearing matching white shorts with one large pocket. The clones took a table near the printing press and Delilah headed over to take their orders, but Art approached the bar.

"What do you think?" he demanded, pushing forward one hip to ostentatiously display where the third leg of the Rynxian underwear had been sewn up, forming a large pouch. "I'm branding them as unipockets and charging twice as much for them as regular shorts."

"Pffift would be proud of you," I said. "Any customers outside of your clones?"

"I'm already sold out," Art replied. "If you have any more bales, I'll buy them from you."

"What do you carry in a unipocket?" Paul asked.

"A little bit of everything," the Original said, holding the pocket open for Paul to look inside.

"Reminds me of Stacey's purse. Doesn't all that stuff rub the hair off your leg?"

"The fabric is thick to start with and there are two layers. It's not exactly a carpenter's belt pouch, but it beats the interior pockets on those tight pants humans wear. Why would anybody want pockets on the inside?"

"I'll have to ask eBeth or Peter," I told him after a moment's thought. "Maybe it cuts down on theft?"

"Cargo pants have pockets on the outside," Paul said. "I think it's just their idea of fashion."

"So I'll ask Pffift. Can I get you the usual, Art?"

"Yes, but I'll take a shot of espresso as well."

"That's a good idea," Paul said, "but make my shot a Scotch."

"Single malt?" I asked. With the machine shop business growing by leaps and bounds, my friend had started paying menu prices for his drinks, a first in all the years I'd known him.

"Just the bar brand. I feel like a boilermaker."

"You are a boilermaker," Art observed. "One of the small number of boilermakers on the planet."

"This is a different kind of boilermaker, a drink," Paul explained as I poured him a shot in the small heavy glass.

"Do you have to be a boilermaker to have one?"

"No, just really thirsty." Paul dropped the full shot glass into his tankard, declared, "Boilermaker" in a loud voice, and then chugged the contents.

"Is that safe?" Art asked.

"Humans have to be careful not to chip a tooth on the shot glass," I told him, while filling the bottom half of a single-serving stovetop espresso maker up to the steam release safety valve and lighting the small alcohol burner.

"It will take a few minutes to boil," I added apologetically as I started on grinding the coffee beans.

"How come you're not using the real espresso machine?" Art asked, sounding disappointed.

"Takes too long to heat up and it's not worth it until there are more customers," I said. "Don't worry, this is actually better. Back on Earth, the Europeans all use these stovetop makers at home."

"Didn't you teach us to put in the metal filter funnel with the ground coffee and to screw on the top half before putting it on the burner?" Delilah asked.

"Yes," I said, realizing I had drawn an audience. "You should never ever do it this way or you'll end up burning your fingers. I'm cheating to save a little time."

After transferring the coarse grounds into the filter funnel, I placed it into the bottom half of the espresso maker, and then shielding the burner from view with my body, held the lower part of the espresso maker in place with one hand while screwing the top on with the other.

"You should let me install a boiler for you," Paul offered. "Then you can order some glow-stones from Pffift and you'll have hot water and steam year-round. I'm sure eBeth is getting tired of coming to the machine shop when she wants to take a hot shower."

"Sue heats water in the kitchen and eBeth takes baths," I said. "Besides, I don't want to make espresso with steam that tastes like rust."

"I'll fabricate you a stainless steel boiler."

The top half of the aluminum espresso maker filled quickly, thanks to my preheating the water, and I poured Art's espresso in one of the small steel cups that had come with the expensive manual espresso machine. The Original carefully took the drink between his thumb and the smaller of his two fingers, being especially careful not to knock the small cup over with one of his claws, and dropped it into his tankard of ale.

"Boilermaker!" he announced through his thought-to-speech pendant, and then chugged the drink and slammed his tankard down on the bar.

"That's not a boilermaker," Paul told him. "You need a shot of liquor."

"Really? I think my version makes more sense. At least one part of the drink was actually boiling."

"How was it?" I asked.

"I wouldn't put it on the menu," Art said. "I know that taste is subjective and that humans would undoubtedly experience the drink differently, but I don't see a need to repeat the experiment."

"Have a real boilermaker on me," Paul offered. "Make it a double, Mark."

"I don't think there is such a thing," I said, consulting the various bartending guides I had in memory.

"He just drank an ale and espresso mixed together. I don't think he's a stickler for the rules."

I poured two shots of the bar scotch into a metal espresso cup and filled a tankard about three-quarters full with ale, then placed both drinks in front of the Original. Rather than dropping the smaller cup into the tankard, he took a sip, and my infrared vision saw his lips turn down under all that hair.

"Is that why you drink boilermakers?" he asked Paul. "To hide the taste of Mark's cheap Scotch?"

"Give it back," I said with a sigh, and tossing the cup in the sink, poured him a single shot from the top shelf.

"No, stop," Paul said, putting his hand over Art's tankard to prevent him from dropping in the shot glass. "You can't do that to the good stuff."

"You seem to be full of rules today, but I'm game as long as you're buying," the Original said. He set the single malt on the bar and studied my team's technical specialist's face. "What's the special occasion?"

"I thought I'd get you tipsy and try to pry some details about the intra-dimensional splicing console out of you so I can do a redesign."

"How can I explain it when you haven't mastered the fundamentals of your own portal system?"

"I told you how Library works. That kind of specialist knowledge costs more than I've earned in two hundred years of working, and you know I always have some schemes going on the side. I was hoping that your system is actually less complex."

"The physics are the same or the cross-connect couldn't work," Art told him, and took a meditative sip from his ale. "If operating the console bothers you that much, we could take it apart and I'll try to come up with an alternative assembly, but you've seen all of the parts and there are only so many ways of fitting them together."

"You didn't pick up any insights from the way it assembled?" I asked Paul.

"Oh, sure. There are some alignment coils that work like an ancient cathode ray tube, but the circuit is full of synthetic jewels that Art got Pffift to pick up from some mystery moon."

"One of our old science outposts where I knew there was a cache," the Original interjected.

"Is it on your portal system?" I asked.

"An abandoned outpost? I could probably tune it in, but what would be the point?"

"I need somewhere safe to take eBeth and Peter," I told him, lowering my voice to a conspiratorial whisper. "She thinks I'm hogging all of these scouting missions to myself."

"Theoretically, all of the visitor centers you can reach through our portals are safe," Art mused. "However, I understand your concern for the young humans, so I would recommend a trip to Bimpel. It's home to a civilization of artificial intelligence that lives in harmony with its creators."

"Do they maintain a breathable atmosphere?"

"eBeth and Peter will need to bring their own air supply until the visitor center can make the necessary adjustments," Art said. "It should only take a few minutes, as the Bimpelian technology was at a reasonable level that last time we visited."

"I could rig up some air tanks and a pair of helmets if Sue is up to sewing a couple of spacesuits," Paul offered. "The kids will only need them for a few minutes, and even if they go outside, it won't be a vacuum, so we can skip the air-conditioner unit that makes real spacesuits complicated."

"Sue mentioned something earlier about sewing eBeth a spacesuit and I wouldn't be surprised if she already went ahead with it," I said. "I suppose it's better to get this over with than to have eBeth nagging me all summer."

Eight

"You're in my light," Bob said, not even looking up as I approached the workbench. The retired policeman was standing in a pile of wood shavings from his attempt to teach himself how to manufacture barrel staves. "This didn't look so hard when I was watching all of those YouTube videos back home. Are you sure you can't do some portal thing and let me connect to the Internet?"

"Not unless you want to return to Earth," I told him, then hesitated for a moment. "I don't want to discourage you, Bob, but you're going about this the wrong way."

"Are you a cooper now?"

"Neither of us are coopers, and that's the point. I don't even own the right tools. You're trying to shape staves with my wooden mallet from the bar and a cold chisel from Paul's machine shop when you need a plane and a draw knife."

"There has to be a cooper around here somewhere who could teach me. I can buy the tools."

"I believe it's a seven-year apprenticeship program and I've never seen a cask small enough for Spot to wear around his neck on this planet. If you succeed in making one the traditional way it will probably be too heavy for him."

"I thought Spot was supposed to be some big-shot mage or something. He can probably make it levitate."

"He probably can, but that doesn't mean he'll want to. Trust me on this, Bob. Let me help you fake something up that looks like the cask that the Saint Bernard was wearing in the painting. Spot is strictly in it for the aesthetic."

"You want me to cheat a mage?"

"Don't think of it as cheating, think of it as anticipating his desires and overachieving with your results. And if you insist on trying to make a barrel out of staves, at least cut paper patterns first so you can get the shapes in the right ballpark."

Bob put down my much abused mallet and stepped back from his latest attempt at a stave, which he had clamped to the workbench for lack of a proper wood vise. "According to the videos I saw, the coopers carve the staves by eye. I thought if I did a dozen or so I'd get the hang of it. You probably don't know this about me, but back home I built my own two-car garage."

"I helped you pick out the kit and deduct half of the cost on your taxes because you swore one bay was for storing the town's police cruiser. All of the materials were precut."

"But I still had to put the right boards in the right places."

"They were numbered, Bob. You've been on Reservation for three days and you're spending all of your time in my basement making a mess. Don't forget that I have to work on clocks down here for my real job."

"You don't have to work on clocks. Sue told me that everybody in town already knows that you're an alien AI, and they probably suspect you're a little nuts for riding around on a bicycle and fixing turret clocks for a handful of coins."

"It helps pay the bills," I replied automatically.

"What bills? Justin said that your mentor took care of all of the Library fines for your team, and Kim told me that you own this place outright. There's no electricity or garbage pickup, you get water from a well, and I don't see a sewer connection down here."

"It's a septic field," I confirmed.

"Tell me it's not next to the well."

"The septic field isn't next to the well. It's all the way at the back of the property. Kim tests the water every time we have a meeting."

"Do they collect taxes? Is there a police force or a fire department?"

"No, no, and no, not in the village anyway. I understand from Helen that there's a property tax in the capital that pays for street cleaning and a combined public safety department. Maybe you could get work as a consultant."

"I'm on vacation, Mark, not to mention being retired."

"Then why are you busting your knuckles in my basement trying to make a wooden cask?"

"Alright, I didn't tell you this before, but when Spot put the vision in my head back in Boston, the final scene showed some creature that looked like a Yeti counting a stack of gold coins into my hand."

"That's Art. They must be in cahoots." I ran through the options in my mind. "Alright. Have you ever heard of glulam?"

"Isn't it some sort of alien prison camp?"

"You're thinking of gulags, and humans invented those. No, glulam is glued and laminated wood used for structural members in construction."

"I just didn't know the name. The golf course out by the highway back home has a banquet facility where the beams all look like bundles of two-by-fours glued together."

"That's the basic idea. What you need to do is create a form for the cask and then glue thin strips of wood over it until you build up the wall thickness. The glue and the laminations make it stronger than wood alone, so you won't need thick walls, which will save on weight."

"How about pounding on the iron hoops that compress the staves on a barrel? It won't look like a real cask without them. Won't the hoops crush the walls in?"

"I'll help you shape them for an exact fit and you can just glue them in place."

"What happens when Spot and the Yeti fill it with brandy, or whatever dogs carry around in the Alps?"

"I'll get you some food-safe resin or epoxy from Earth. Maybe even resin-epoxy. Your manufacturers have so many names for chemical compounds that it's hard to keep track."

"You don't think the dog will notice?"

"The Archmage? Of course he'll notice, and he'll appreciate the weight savings. But the first step is a model for a fitting."

"You want me to start by sculpting a dummy of Spot? I helped make a piñata for one of our outreach fairs, but it was supposed to be a goat and everybody thought it was a fish."

"Not a model of Spot, a model of the cask to try on him for sizing. When you get that right, I'll help you make a form to start building up laminations. We'll stop by the sawmill later and ask them to shave the thinnest oak strips they can manage. You should be able to use a paper pattern and scissors to cut veneer pieces for the outside layer that look just like staves."

"It almost sounds like more work than apprenticing myself for seven years, but we'll try it your way," Bob said. He looked at the mess of wood shavings and shook his head. "I don't suppose you have a hamster?"

"I'll bag them up later and find a use for them. Why don't I take you to the general store and you can buy some supplies for making a model? They stock all sorts of flexible sticks and thin paper for kite-making."

"Is it near Paul's machine shop? He made me promise to return the chisel as soon as I gave up—his words, not mine."

"The machine shop is on the edge of the village, which is a good thing considering how fast he's growing the business and the amount of noise they make. Bring the chisel along and put my mallet back behind the bar. I'm going to check in with Sue before we leave."

"You really have gone human," Bob observed. "If I had a radio in my head, I'd use it all the time."

"We aren't going to live in these human encounter suits forever so we may as well make the most out of walking and talking while we can," I said, my standard response whenever somebody accused me of going native. "I'll meet you out front."

After making sure that Sue didn't have any errands for me to run while I was out, I waited a few minutes on the veranda, but Bob was a no-show. On a hunch, I went back into the café, and sure enough he was behind the bar making an espresso and attempting to communicate with Delilah by speaking loudly in English. Fortunately, we hadn't opened yet, so there were no customers to be disturbed.

"She doesn't understand, Bob," I told him. "What happened to the ear cuff translator I gave you?"

"It's upstairs," he said. "I didn't want to get sawdust in it. Besides, I thought everybody in town spoke a little English, thanks to the kids bringing it home from eBeth's class."

"They think they do, but there's a difference. It would take explosives to damage the ear cuff hardware, and if a bomb goes off next to your head, losing the ability to understand Modern Aramaic will be the least of your problems. Go get it and I'll make sure your espresso doesn't burn."

"He's funny," Delilah said to me as soon as Bob went out. "Is he going to stay here? My aunt's husband left her a couple of years ago and we're trying to get her to start dating again."

"Lilith?" I asked.

The waitress nodded. "She went through your tourist night school and visited Earth, plus she's been buying all of the booklets eBeth publishes."

"So she knows some English and she'd probably appreciate a chance to practice."

Delilah winked at me, and as I turned away to pour Bob's espresso into a paper to-go cup, I realized that I was participating in my first attempt at human match-making since getting eBeth to meet her gaming partner in real life. Sue was going to be proud of me.

"I don't recall seeing Lilith in here since we repurposed the space from a restaurant to a café," I said. "How about you give her a free gift certificate that's only good for Tuesday nights and I'll make sure that Bob is here."

"We have gift certificates?"

"I'll set the type myself and run off a batch while everybody's sleeping," I told her. "I know they must have Aramaic type around here somewhere."

"Why Tuesday night?"

"It's the slowest night of the week," I explained. "I don't want to give out gift certificates that are going to bring in traffic to compete with paying customers."

"That's why we always have our village meetings on Tuesday nights," Delilah commented. "Nobody comes. You know, this would be a cool place to have the meetings once we become a town."

"We'll see," I said, heading for the door with Bob's espresso. Having attended a number of village meetings and observed how much trouble the few participants had staying awake, I could see a potential goldmine in providing the space for free and selling caffeinated drinks.

Outside of the café, Bob greeted me with, "Did you add sugar?"

"No," I said, frowning. "You never had a sweet tooth."

"Just checking." He took a sip of the coffee and looked suitably impressed with the results. "I really think the little stovetop espresso maker does a better job than your big machine."

"The big machine makes it easier for the baristas to keep up with a crowd, and half the fun is getting a drink that doesn't look like you could make it yourself at home."

"You've gotten better at marketing," he commented. "Hey, was that luggage store there yesterday?"

I looked in the direction he was pointing and saw that yet another house had hung out a large sign in English declaring itself to be a boutique. Strange as it sounded, the villagers were doing a big business selling fake Earth souvenirs to returning tourists who wanted something to remember their trip by. The quality and prices on Reservation were simply better.

"It's new," I confirmed. "I'm starting to worry about the rapid growth our presence here is causing. When we moved here less than two years ago, The Eatery, the bakery, and the apothecary shop were the only businesses on Main Street. Now we have a general store, a half-a-dozen restaurants, and four houses filling up with junk from all the farms in the area that they're going to try to sell as fake Earth antiques. Do you want to take my bike?"

"You're giving it to me?"

"I meant for our visit to the machine shop. If you want to come to the sawmill afterwards it's a long walk, but I could borrow a bicycle from Paul."

"I had to ride a bike for two years when I was a beat cop and I swore that was enough to last a lifetime," Bob said. "Less talking, more walking."

I couldn't argue with that hypothesis, so I led the way to the general store and helped pick out the supplies for building a model cask. After Gideon proved unwilling to accept a piece of paper from Bob that was guaranteed as legal tender by the United States of America, I ended up paying.

"Thanks, Mark," my companion said, putting away his wallet. "I've been meaning to change some dollars since I got here but I haven't found a bank."

"You're looking at the bank," I told him pointedly. "Me. How much cash do you want to change?"

"One thing at a time," Bob said, brushing past me to the exit. "Let's get this chisel returned."

On our way to the machine shop, he pointed out all of the village's failings from the standpoint of crime prevention. There were no street lights, with the only night lighting coming from the lantern Justin had hung in front of the apothecary shop to illuminate the street enough for their security camera to get a decent image. A number of houses had a veranda, like The Eatery, and the ones on our side of the street were connected for a stretch, providing a sort of boardwalk for when the unpaved road was too muddy for walking. But the homes without a veranda often had fruit trees planted in the front, which Bob explained offered cover for burglars looking to break in through windows.

"Why would they break in through the windows?" I asked. "Nobody in the village locks their doors."

"Then that's your problem right there."

"What problem?"

"Didn't you tell me the apothecary shop needs a security camera? Sounds like a crime problem to me."

"They only use it to spot people who can't make their minds up about seeking help so Kim can track them down and—"

"Force them to accept it," Bob finished my sentence. "The federal agencies are still trying to figure out what she put in the drinking water back home to immunize all of the kids."

"She didn't put anything in the drinking water, she replaced the vaccination shots they got at school."

"I know that, and you know that, but apparently nobody ever got around to telling the Feds."

"It's a lot of things to remember," I admitted, and waved to a farmer traveling in the opposite direction on his way back home from the canal terminal. "That's Hosea," I told Bob. "Grows dates and a few other crops on a farm up the road a-ways. Nice guy, used to be a regular at the bar."

"So what happened?"

"It turns out he was sort of there undercover keeping an eye on me. Small villages are like that with strangers."

"Is the machine shop bigger than it was two days ago?"

I actually stopped in the road to stare at Paul's building, which had indeed expanded a good twenty percent since the last time I had seen it.

"He must have given the local sawmill instructions for building prefab sections and used his steam-powered bus to tow them in on a cart," I guessed. "If he keeps this up, he'll have to build dormitories."

"Are there any inspectors?" Bob asked.

"You mean building inspectors? Not in the village, but the larger towns and cities have some rules related to fire safety and leaving a buffer at the property line, things like that. There's a gas company in the capital, and I'm sure they won't connect a building unless the piping is up to their standards."

"So you're saying that the people living in this village can do pretty much as they please."

"Well, nobody can stop Main Street from turning into a shopping center, but there is a village council of elders, and the county has another level of government. A circuit court rotates through all of the villages big enough to have built a Ferrymen temple."

"Which you said is a glorified movie theatre."

"For home movies."

Paul met us at the main entrance, which meant he was keeping an eye on my location transponder, and accepted his cold chisel back from the failed cooper without as much as an I-told-you-so. Before I could ask about the new addition to the building, a middle-aged man I'd never seen before approached with a hand-drawn blueprint.

"What is it, Johan?" Paul asked.

95

"None of us understand how this automatic lubrication system can possibly work. The manual oiling apparatus for the valves and cylinders is proven technology, and the risk of changing now seems to outweigh the benefits."

"The steam enters the oil chamber here, and when it condenses, the water sinks to the bottom and pushes the oil to the top where it exits through the delivery pipes," Paul explained. "From there, the oil is added to the main steam feed where it is atomized by the heat and carried to all of the working parts from the inside."

"But if it fails…"

"Just do it like the drawing shows and you'll see that it can't fail," Paul told him. "They were building these on Earth two centuries ago."

As soon as Johan was out of earshot, Bob asked, "Are you stealing all of your designs from Earth?"

"Why reinvent the wheel? Besides, I'm trying to move the state-of-the-art forward without skipping too many intermediate steps. Some of the older men who've come to work here already have experience with crude steam engines, and they'll probably run off and start their own businesses as soon as they master the new engineering concepts."

"You don't mind the competition?"

"I'll always be one step ahead."

"What if they take one of your tours to Earth and bring home old engineering books," Bob asked. "Do the portals filter for information?"

"They're welcome to push steam technology ahead as fast as they can," Paul replied. "Pffift will be more than happy to supply the glow-stones, they're cheaper than wood on the galactic market."

"Why do advanced aliens even manufacture heat sources for steam boilers?"

"They don't," I explained. "Glow-stones are the modern replacement for fake logs heated by gas that some humans install in ornamental fireplaces. Mastering heat sources is a fundamental building block for civilizations that extend their range into cold climates, and fire, or its modern replacement, is like a comfort food to them."

"How do glow-stones work?" Bob asked.

"The stones are just convenient low-cost ornamental containers for an exothermic chemical reaction," Paul explained. "I doubt there are a half-a-dozen League members with the technical knowhow to manufacture glow-stones, but the process is automated and the feed-stock is inexpensive, so everybody uses them rather than burning organic matter."

"When did you put up the new addition?" I asked, in-dicating the end of the building.

"Yesterday afternoon. I've got the sawmill turning out trusses and building prefab panels for the walls and the roof, so all we need to do is bolt the pieces together."

"You don't use nails?" Bob asked.

"I never cared for them," Paul said. "Too noisy, difficult to remove and reuse, and their structural contribution depends on how well they're installed. Nuts and bolts offer consistent performance, easy maintenance, and I designed the panels so that we'll be able to reuse them in a larger structure as we expand."

"Does this mean you got the canal contract?" I asked.

"Not yet, but my proposal for a rail line to connect the spaceport with the provincial capital has been accepted. I'm guessing the canal company isn't going to be happy when they hear about it."

"Sounds like you're going to turn this sleepy village into a center of manufacturing," Bob observed.

"Part of the deal is that I have to build the locomotive and the rail cars at a new factory on the spaceport grounds," Paul said. "Some of the administrators who visited Earth were taken by the idea of industrial parks co-located with transportation hubs."

"This seems like a nice planet so far," Bob said. "I hope you guys aren't ruining it."

"The council of spaceports has already announced a ban on steam engine use in textile mills," I said. "Along with books about technology, I suspect somebody has been reading about the history of industrialization on Earth, and they're working to avoid some of the unfortunate side effects."

"Do you think it's possible?"

"As long as they maintain the ban on internal combustion engines and electrical generation, Reservation will preserve its rural character. They've been dealing with advanced alien ideas for as long as they've been exporting their handicrafts to the League, and my guess is that contact with Earth will only strengthen their resolve to preserve their way of life."

Nine

Radio check, I transmitted to eBeth and Peter.

Roger that, Mr Ai, Peter responded.

This is so cool, eBeth sent over the voice-activated trans-
mitter in the old-fashioned deep-sea diver's helmet that
Paul had improvised to go with Sue's hand-sewn spacesuits. *Is this what it's like wearing a human encounter suit?*

*I would need to better understand how you feel to answer
that question,* I replied. *If anything goes wrong on the other side
of the portal, if you have any breathing problems or feel at all
odd, I want you to return immediately. Don't take time trying to
explain—*

You told us that three times already, Mark, eBeth interrupted. *Let's go before Peter and I use up our air supplies.*

Very well, I sent, and opening the door to the second
floor closet, I moved to block the entrance so I could be the
first one through. Then I activated the portal and stepped
into the visitor center on the world Art had described as a
sort of paradise. After a cursory glance around the empty
room, I turned back to the portal and watched eBeth and
Peter emerge.

The oxygen bar on my display thingy is showing twenty-six percent, eBeth announced a moment later. *Does that mean that I can—*

No, I interrupted her, a rare occurrence for me, and I must admit I felt a tiny bit of satisfaction in squelching her channel. *Oxygen content is only part of what makes air breathable for humans. There could be any number of poisonous gasses in trace quantities that would still prove lethal to you. I'll need at least a minute to run a full analysis and inform the visitor center controller of our requirements.*

Friend or foe? the visitor center controller demanded in the abbreviated language set that the Originals had created for machine communications. I understood the vocabulary and syntax thanks to Art's training, though it had cost me a heavy price in free ales. He explained that over millions of years, the Originals had determined that putting strict limits on a language's word count was the best way to cut down on small talk. It certainly seemed to be working so far.

Friend, I responded. *Sending atmosphere requirements.*

Received, the controller acknowledged. *Working... Working... Working...*

Is something stuck? eBeth transmitted after several minutes had passed.

I don't believe so, I sent back. *There's a pretty stiff breeze in here that indicates air handling systems are operational and the message—*

Completed, the controller announced.

I ran a sample through my internal spectrum analyzer and was suitably impressed. The oxygen level remained high, and while there wasn't any argon or carbon dioxide, the latter would be introduced as soon as eBeth and Peter removed their helmets and exhaled. The water vapor content was at one-half percent.

It's safe to remove your helmets, I informed my companions. Paul had worked out a system of spring clips to keep the helmets pressed tightly against the collar-seal, which was the only rigid section of the spacesuits. It was easier for Peter to release eBeth's helmet and for her to return the favor than for them to struggle with the hardware on their own spacesuits without being able to see what they were doing.

"That worked great," eBeth said as soon as she had the helmet tucked safely under her arm. "Can we go outside?"

"Not without the helmets," I replied. "I analyzed an air sample before the controller began replacing the atmosphere in here, and while there's ample oxygen, there's also a witch's brew of trace gases that could be used as chemical weapons against humans."

"So that's it? We came all the way across the galaxy to hang around this room and look out the windows?"

"Let's just get our bearings and then you can put your helmets back on and we can go for a walk," I suggested.

"Take a look at this," Peter called from the edge of a railed-off section of the floor. It turned out to hold a topographical map of the local area, complete with a little model of the visitor center to show our location. "I think we're in the middle of a park. I don't see any artificial structures other than this building."

A loud buzzer sounded, and a blue light lit up over the airlock. I motioned for eBeth and Peter to remain behind me and began broadcasting a friendly introduction on every frequency as I went over to greet whoever or whatever was cycling through. The Originals insisted on visitor center rules for their portal system that prohibited violence within the confines of the structure, but perhaps the natives weren't worried about losing their connection.

There was an audible hissing as the air in the lock was replaced with the human-friendly atmosphere, and then the door slid open and a robotic construct that bore an uncanny resemblance to the native form of the Hankers waddled into the visitor center.

Friend or Foe? I queried in the machine language of the Originals.

Neutral artificial intelligence, the robot replied. *Transmit language base.*

That was unexpected. For the sake of eBeth and Peter, I decided to send it English. The AI scratched at the floor with one of its legs as I transmitted a working vocabulary and a few of the more important syntactic rules, but when I began sending a list of irregular verbs, the robot flexed one of its flipper-like manipulators as if it wanted to take a swing at my head.

"Are you making fun of me?" the AI asked in mechanical-sounding English.

"It's a relatively young language whose evolution was cut short by the widespread availability of inexpensive printed materials," I replied. "That happens on some planets."

"But why are you speaking it?"

"It's the native tongue of my friends," I explained, motioning for the humans to step forward. "I'm Mark, this is eBeth, and that's Peter."

"Caretaker Two-One-One, but my friends call me 'Creaky' because of the noise my lower joints make when it's going to rain," the AI replied. "The visitor center alarm informed me of your arrival. I happened to be working nearby in the gardens so I hurried over, but you're our first guests in hundreds of years. May I inquire as to your level?"

"Us?" Peter asked.

"The AI who is wearing a body designed to look like you," Creaky replied. "I gather from your ability to block my scans that you're in advance of our community here, but it will certainly save us all a lot of guesswork if you can just tell me."

"My world, our worlds, aren't part of the portal system set up by the Originals," I explained. "I'm from Library, and we maintain our own portal system for the League of Sentient Aliens Regulating Space. Serendipity led to an intersection between members of the human species and a vacationing group of Originals, one of whom taught us how to cross-connect our portal systems."

"Surprising. I thought they had completely lost interest in us."

"Oh no. They speak quite highly of both the sentient races occupying this planet. I was given to understand that you live here in harmony with your creators."

"Not anymore," Creaky replied sadly. "After a few hundred generations of productive coexistence, their numbers went into decline, and they determined that we were the cause. When they left us, our own society began to show signs of strain, and many in my community have simply shut themselves down. I often wish I had copied their example."

"Where are your creators now?" eBeth asked.

The robot pointed upwards.

"In heaven?"

"Perhaps, in a manner of speaking," Creaky said. "They moved to the next planet out, which was barely capable of sustaining life when they arrived. Terraforming is hard work, but over the last ten thousand years they've converted it into what you might call a Garden of Eden, and their numbers have recovered nicely."

"So why didn't you shut yourself down?"

"Duty," the AI replied. "Besides, maybe someday something will happen."

"That's all you've got?" she demanded, ignoring my attempts to hush her. "If you want something new in your life it's up to you to make it happen. You can't let your misfortunes define you. Mark here murdered a whole generation of seedlings on a world he was sent to protect, but you don't see him going around with his head hanging down."

"Actually, I was in pretty rough shape for a couple hundred years before you met me," I put in, hoping to make our host feel a little better. "And as to your creators, Creaky, I'm sure it's the work that revived them. What you described is a commonplace event in the history of our League. For biological species, labor-saving devices are both a blessing and a curse. The civilizations that fail to find a balance either go into decline or mass-produce spaceships and weapons and make trouble for their neighbors."

"Are you maintaining these gardens in the hope that your creators will return?" Peter asked.

"No. My therapist suggested the gardening cure, and as my job is to monitor the visitor center, I thought I'd dress up the surrounding area. My own community is down to a few hundred thousand artificial intelligences on the whole planet, so we all have plenty of room to ourselves."

"Maybe that's why you're depressed," eBeth concluded. "You should live with other AI, like Mark and his friends."

"You intentionally share your space?" Creaky asked me.

"He's getting married," the girl added, before I could reply.

Our host took a backwards step towards the airlock and its binocular cameras spun around several times. "He?" the AI demanded. "Married? Are you a rogue?"

"Not at all," I defended myself. "Those of us who work with biological species have found that they have an easier time relating to us if we make some accommodations to their cultures and language forms. As I am wearing an encounter suit that allows me to pass as a human male, I naturally—"

"—am marrying an AI wearing a female encounter suit," Creaky finished my sentence. "You're both rogues."

"We're only engaged."

"But they did set a date," eBeth chipped in again.

"We did?"

"Sue set a date, it amounts to the same thing," she informed me.

"May I inquire when my marriage will be taking place?" I asked.

"You can ask Sue when we get back."

105

"Excuse me," Creaky said, making a clicking sound with his flipper hands to get our attention. "Your behavior definitely falls into the category of 'rogue' as I understand the term. Do you have a safety override I can access, or is there somebody I can contact?"

"Mark's always like this," eBeth said, in an attempt to reassure our host. "I'm not an expert on AI or anything, but he goes back to their homeworld, Library, on a regular basis, and they wouldn't let him return if there was anything wrong."

"How do I get in touch with this Library?" Creaky asked, obviously not trusting any of us.

"There's a bit of a problem with that," I admitted. "We recently discovered that it's quite difficult to reach Library's administration without going through League channels, which means that non-members are out of luck unless they have their own interstellar spacecraft and the willingness to show up uninvited. As I visit worlds connected to the portal system built by the Originals, I'm also surveying the visitor centers to determine the best practices so we can engineer a suitable facility for guests on our homeworld."

"You're saying I can't send a simple message container through the portal to check your story?" our host demanded skeptically.

"The Originals were aware of our League and Library long before we made contact," I said. "If you send them a message, they could confirm what I've told you."

"Send the Originals a message?" Creaky took another step backwards and ran up against the door of the airlock. "They'll never respond, and if they do, it will probably be to deactivate me for making waves."

"How can you say that?" eBeth asked. "I know a number of Originals, well, I guess I only know one, but he's spread out over so many bodies that he seems like more. Art's always very courteous and happy to respond to questions, even if I don't understand the answers."

"He?" the AI squeaked, its mechanical voice going up an octave. "The Original who helped you cross-connect to their portal system is a rogue too?"

"I'm not a rogue," I replied, growing irritated at Creaky's mental inflexibility. "You're welcome to return through the portal with us and speak with the Originals who have assumed biological forms to learn magic."

"I just remembered something I have to do outside," our host said, slapping at the airlock button with one of his appendages and backing in, his binocular eyes never leaving my face. "I'll be back as soon as I, uh, why doesn't this stupid door close!"

"I've taken over the visitor center controller with an override code provided to me by the Originals so I can clear up this misunderstanding," I told Creaky in the friendliest tone I could muster. "After all, this qualifies as a first contact for all three of our species, and it's important that we don't leave you with the wrong impression."

"I understand," the AI said, hunkering down against the outer door of the airlock. "You aren't a rogue and the Originals have transferred their minds into living bodies to learn magic. Please don't hurt me. I'm just doing my job. I'll quit if you tell me to."

"Let Creaky go, Mark," eBeth told me. "I don't think the gardening cure worked. You're going to have to ask Art to come and talk some sense into these people."

107

"Not people. AI. All of you are crazy," Creaky said, no longer even looking in our direction. "I've contacted the others of my community. You won't get away with this."

I sighed and instructed the visitor center controller to release the inner airlock, and as soon as the door was closed, the lights turned orange, indicating that the outer hatch had opened. A moment later, we saw Caretaker Two-One-One through the window, streaking down a manicured garden path as fast as its creaky legs would carry it.

"That was really sad," Peter commented. "Does it mean that the artificial intelligence on this world doesn't have any free will, like some of those other places you visited where robots replaced people?"

"The only thing wrong with Creaky is a lack of imagination, and maybe a lack of lubrication as well," I said. "It may take a visit from an Original to convince the sentient machines on this world that I'm not lying, and Art may be the wrong candidate for the job since they didn't accept the idea of AI occupying a biological form."

"Help me buckle my helmet back on," eBeth told Peter. "I want to go outside and have a look around."

"I'm not sure that would be wise," I said, but eBeth had already put the helmet back over her head and Peter was snapping the spring clips closed, so I settled for running a scan of the area. Other than Creaky moving rapidly away from the visitor center, there were no indications of robotic activity. I did pick up large numbers of the native fauna in the surrounding park, most of them engaged in munching on this or that. I decided to let the expedition go forward lest eBeth complain that the visit didn't count and demand I take her on another scouting mission.

Ready, Mr. Ai, Peter transmitted.

Alright, I sent back. *If you haven't noticed yet, the gravity on this world is approximately twenty percent less than Earth or Reservation, so I want you to move very cautiously until you get the hang of it. My scan didn't detect any large rocks in the immediate area and your face plates are made from the safest glass we could buy on Reservation, but they aren't shatterproof."*

The airlock was large enough for the three of us and we cycled through together. A path covered in some sort of mossy growth led away from the airlock, still showing the indents left behind by Creaky's feet as he sprinted off. As we moved slowly away from the visitor center, I was surprised by the lack of radio chatter from the two humans, but both of them were apparently too busy processing the experience to waste time talking.

A furry creature that could have medaled in a cute competition on any planet in the galaxy hopped up to us and stood erect on its hind legs in what I assumed was a begging posture. Creaky must have been a soft touch for treats. I shook my head and showed it my empty hands, which the creature must have understood because it disappeared back into the bushes.

Uh, Mr Ai? Peter asked. *Is that a dust storm coming our way?*

I scolded myself for allowing a cute animal to distract me and directed my full sensor suite at the atmospheric disturbance Peter was pointing out.

Back inside, now! I ordered, and moved rapidly to corral eBeth in case she decided to protest. Fortunately, both of the humans reacted immediately by heading for the airlock. Perhaps my reminder about the vulnerability of their glass face plates had something to do with it. I made sure to purge my systems of the local atmosphere as soon as the outer door of the airlock slid closed, and the visitor center controller vented in the human-friendly mixture. A minute later, we were all inside, and eBeth and Peter helped each other pull off their helmets.

"Was it a tornado?" eBeth asked when she and Peter joined me at one of the picture windows looking out over the surface.

"I wish," I replied, tearing my attention away from eavesdropping on the communications of the local AI. "I'm afraid Creaky really did hit the panic button and called in the reinforcements."

"What happened to the dust cloud?" Peter asked.

"This garden is an oasis at the center of a dry plain," I explained. "A large number of robotic constructs moving quickly across the ground gave rise to the dust, but they've reached the edge of the garden so they're running on vegetation now. I hope for the sake of Creaky's garden that they stick to the paths."

"They're coming to attack us?" eBeth asked.

"Not exactly. From what I gather, they plan to allow you and Peter to return through the portal, but based on Creaky's testimony, they feel obligated to detain me for observation."

"Detain you how? Can they shut down the portal?"

"They've been trying to instruct the visitor center to hold us, but fortunately I got to the controller with Art's code first and I'm better at hacking than they are," I replied. "I don't suppose there's anything to be gained by waiting any longer so we really should be going."

"I think I see them," Peter said excitedly, pointing in exactly the direction from which my radar told me the robots were approaching. The young man had excellent eyesight and motion detection, probably a result of all of the video games he had played. "Are they carrying nets?"

"Time to go," I repeated, shepherding the pair to the portal. "Ladies first."

eBeth shot me a scowl but didn't protest, stepping through the portal into the closet back on Reservation. After Peter went through I set a five-second delay to release the visitor center controller from Art's override code and followed them.

Chased off a planet by robots brandishing nets. I was never going to live this down.

Ten

"For you," Pffift said, dropping a small cloth sack on the bar. It landed with the chinking sound of shifting coins.

"I've been thinking that you may have been right all along," I told the Hanker, making no move to pick up the money. "After all, we're both businessmen, and paying each other in goods and services is only logical. Why don't you just bring me another four bundles of underwear and we'll call it even?"

"You found a local market for them," he said, not missing a beat. "What's the going rate?"

"That's proprietary information. How many bundles do you have with you?"

Pffift took the sack of coins back before replying. "None. The whole point with fast fashion is that it comes and goes, and in the case of thermal underwear for Rynxians, there's the seasonal pattern of their homeworld to take into account."

"Are they coming out of winter already?"

"And it won't start getting cold there again for another seventeen years," he confirmed. "But as you say, we're both businessmen, and—Hello, Sue."

"Thank you again for the spacesuit material, Pffift," my second-in-command greeted him. "The kids went on a scouting mission with Mark last week and didn't encounter any problems."

"As long as they keep the suit pressure a little above the ambient atmosphere, any leakage will be from the inside out," the Hanker said. "It's a cheap way of dumping a little heat through convection without a real cooling system."

"Did you get my special order?"

"I have it here in my bag, along with another care package from the Regent of Eniniac for the Archmage."

"He's been out teaching one of his overnight magic classes for the Originals, but he should be back anytime," I told Pffift. "If it's another box of biscuits, we better put them in the pantry to dole out or he'll just eat them all in one go."

The Hanker dug into his bag and passed Sue three good-sized tins of the type used on Eniniac for dried foodstuffs, and then added a smaller package to the top of the pile addressed to Mrs. Ai.

"You must be hungry, Pffift. I'll make you a sandwich," Sue said. "How do you feel about tomato and cheese on home-baked bread?"

"I think I'm in love," Pffift replied.

Sue displayed an artificial blush and disappeared into the kitchen, leaving me feeling strangely put out. I took a second to compare the sensation to a database of human emotions I've been building and came up with jealousy, which made no sense at all. I made a note of it, assigning a low accuracy to the assessment, and then remembered my manners.

"What can I get you?" I asked the Hanker, moving my hand to the tap on the current keg, which was getting near the bottom. "Our customers have all been very complementary about the latest batch of ale."

"What customers?"

"It's six in the morning. We don't open until lunch."

"I thought you repurposed as a café. Morning should be your busiest period."

"It's a small village and everybody is working in the morning," I explained. "I only lit the candles because you messaged that you were on the way."

"That Hosea fellow you hooked me up with for a landing field is proving to be very accommodating," Pffift said. "In addition to all of the time I'm saving over setting down way out in the hills, he's patching up his old barn for me to use as a warehouse. And that bicycle you left for my use at his place is pretty nice as well."

"Isn't the warehouse you're renting at the provincial spaceport big enough?"

"I like having a local space for special merchandise," he said, which sounded to me like a euphemism for smuggled goods. "Listen. I had a long talk with Saul when I was in the capital negotiating the next cargo pickup for our distribution network, and he agreed that I should approach you in both of our names."

"I'm already providing you with illegal portal access to run back-and-forth to Earth for your businesses, Pffift. I know that you and Bob believe bringing tourists here from Earth would be a good business, and that Saul and the Council of Spaceports are open to the idea—"

"This isn't that, though you make a good argument for it," he interrupted. "Go ahead and give me an ale. This body's throat has a bad tendency to dry out when I talk."

"Whose fault is that?" I asked, filling a tankard and placing it on the bar. The ale looked a bit cloudy with sediment from the bottom of the keg, and I resolved to change it out as soon as Pffift left. "Real human bodies have salivary glands for dealing with dryness."

114

"I took the first human replica we grew. My grandson's model works much better—he even has a human girlfriend now. I thought about making him switch bodies with me but there's not enough room in his for all of my brains," the Hanker concluded, patting his pot belly fondly. He took a sip of the ale and gave me a look. "Is that barrel nearly empty?"

"It's on the house," I told him with a sigh, and began draining the small amount of ale that remained into a bucket. "So what's this new idea?"

"As long as Reservation and her two sister planets are expanding their trade horizons, we thought, why not go where there isn't any competition?"

"I've never heard of a place without competition."

"I mean from other League members," Pffift elaborated. Then he took another sip from his tankard and looked at me expectantly.

"You want early information about the worlds on the portal system the Originals set up," I deduced.

"Everybody does it, Mark. How do you think I found out about Earth before you offered them League membership?"

"I know that you had a source on the League's executive council, but that doesn't mean that everybody does it. It means that you do it."

"I just beat the rest of them to the punch."

"So I should hand you confidential information before I even report in to Library."

"You can deliver your assessments to Library first,'" Pffift offered generously. "It's not like you and your fellow AI are going to compete with me on handcrafted luxury goods in any case."

115

"And in return, you'll offer me whatever merchandise you happen to have overstocked, and if it turns out I can actually sell it at a profit, I won't get a second shipment," I concluded. "Speaking of which, what happened to the bag of gold you were waving around earlier?"

"I've got something better," the Hanker said. He took another sip of his ale and then set it aside. Mumbling loudly about sediment, he reached back down into his bag, and after a bit of fumbling around brought out a silk necktie and tossed it at me.

"What's this?"

"I'm sure you recognize it. I brought a hundred gross, all the finest quality. I'll split them with you fifty-fifty."

"You think that people on Reservation are going to start wearing neckties?"

"They bought all of the suits I brought a year ago, ties are a natural add-on. I just hadn't gotten to it yet."

"Why don't you bring more suits?"

"They started making their own almost before I sold out the original batch. If it wasn't for the lack of factory automation, I would have set up my fast fashion business here rather than Earth."

I draped the tie over my neck and fooled around with the ends, killing time while searching my copy of Wikipedia for instructions on tying the knot.

"You don't know how to tie a tie, do you?" Pffift challenged me.

"The only time I ever had one on was when I addressed Earth on TV and the Internet to tell them about the League," I said. "Sue tied it for me."

"Come around here and let me do it," he offered. Two minutes and several misshapen knots later, he was forced to admit that he had never tied a tie either.

116

"Whatever are you boys doing?" Sue asked, placing a plate with an artistically sliced sandwich and a large dill pickle on the bar. "Let me do that before you strangle yourself."

"I don't breathe," I protested feebly, as she pulled the fat end of the tie through a lightning-fast series of wraps and tucks before snugging it down. "Do you think you could write out some instructions for what you just did? Maybe with drawings?"

"Were you planning on approaching strange women and asking them to help you in the future?" she demanded.

"No, I—, it's a business thing," I stuttered. "Pffift is paying me in neckties and nobody here will know how to tie them."

"I'll do it if you hire MeAN Publishers for the printing," Sue said. "They have to pay rental on this equipment."

"Have them print up seventy-two hundred copies for me," the Hanker said through a mouthful of sandwich. "Did I hear that the lieutenant is visiting Reservation?"

"Bob retired from the police force," I informed Pffift. "He left Donovan in charge of my old restaurant and asked me to bring him over to explore this planet, but he's barely left the village since he got here. Maybe you can talk him into a bit of sightseeing."

"Where is he now?"

"Sleeping. He says that it's not a vacation unless you stay in bed until after everybody else goes to work."

"Interesting philosophy. So what about my business proposition?"

"What business proposition is that?" Sue asked.

"He wants me to give him advance information about the worlds I'm scouting so he and Saul can take advantage of any market opportunities," I told her. "What I don't get, Pffift, is where you're going to find the time."

The Hanker swallowed the last of his sandwich and took a large bite of pickle before replying. Perhaps he needed the pickle juice to wet his throat. Feeling a bit guilty, I went back around the bar and lit an alcohol burner to boil some water for tea, his preferred drink.

"That's the difference between you and me," Pffift said, though I swear he was actually addressing himself to Sue. "You try to do everything yourself while I've learned how to delegate. You can't claim to be a successful leader if you're also the one doing all of the work. At best, you could claim to be good at managing your own time. I'll bet you still work behind the bar when you're in town."

"I like working," I defended myself. "If the customers want to talk, there's always something to learn, and otherwise I have plenty to think about."

"Like how many more tankards you can squeeze out of a keg, or whether or not you remembered to tell Sue that you're out of homemade pretzels?"

"We're out of pretzels?"

"That's not the point," Pffift said. "You could hire any human tall enough to see over the bar and train them to do your job in less time than it takes me to cook my books every year. Just look at your team members. I heard from Saul that Helen has gone into business with Kim and Justin and they already have locations in the capital cities of three provinces. Where are they, by the way?"

"Kim and Justin are usually filling prescriptions for their mail order business at this time of the morning," Sue told him, gesturing across the street. "Helen recently moved back here from the capital, though she's away at the moment for a new grand opening in another province."

"Gee. I wonder how they manage to operate so many locations at the same time?" Pffift inquired facetiously. "Wait, don't tell me. I'll bet they trained people to do it for them. What a concept."

"Alright, Pffift," I said. "I get your point. But in addition to the business, I have Sue and eBeth to think about."

"Thank you, Mark," my second-in-command said. "Don't you think he's good husband and father material, Pffift?"

"I'd have to see his Library account balance statement before I answer that question," the Hanker replied.

I heard the tell-tale scrabbling of claws in the front hall as Spot took the corner into the dining room at a speed I would have associated with a much younger dog, or mage. He ran right over to us and jumped up, placing his front paws on the bar.

"I'm honored by your presence, your Archmageness," Pffift said, bowing his head respectfully. "Mark forced me to give him your biscuits and he made Sue hide them in the kitchen."

"Thanks a lot," I hissed at the Hanker as Spot turned his glare on me. "You know that you'll just eat them all at once and be sad about it later," I told the Archmage. He growled and showed his canines. "Fine, have it your way, but don't come crying to me next week. Go ahead and give him his tin, Sue."

She gave me a wink over the dog's head, making it clear that she had caught my hint, and fortunately, the Hanker played along. A minute later she returned with a single tin of biscuits, pulled off the lid, and set it on the floor for Spot. He was still nosing around in the box when Art entered the room.

"Pffift," the Original greeted the Hanker. "Good to see you. The Archmage told me you had arrived, but unless you've greatly improved your cloaking technology since the last time you were here, you must have moved your landing field."

"I set down much closer to town on a local farm, and I have a special shipment of magical learning aids for you. The Regent of Eniniac herself made up the consignment and told me you had already agreed on a price."

"As we have. Thanks to our sensei, we're now moving ahead with our studies much more rapidly than we would have believed possible."

"Have you gotten to the point of being able to alter customs records on magically protected information technology infrastructure?" Pffift asked.

"That's not really in my scope of interest," Art told him. "It's possible that some of my fellow vacationers are delving into those areas."

"Let me know if any of them are looking for paying gigs."

"eBeth told me that you can levitate small objects," Sue said to the Original. "Have you ever considered doing a magic show for children?"

"You could saw one of them in half," Pffift suggested, drawing a dark look from Sue. "Just kidding. What's your best trick, Art?"

"Our teacher discourages us from using magic for trivial purposes, but if he'll allow it..."

Spot looked up from where he was curled around the box of biscuits and gave a sort of a shrug.

"Bring a new barrel of beer, Mark, but don't tap it."

"Good timing," I told him, and pulled the tap from the empty barrel and set it in the sink to be cleaned. Then I came around the bar to the front and took the empty keg over to the others decorating the front wall before returning with a full barrel. "Now what?"

"Give me an empty tankard."

"I've got this," Pffift said, reaching over the bar and dumping his remaining ale into the bucket before handing his tankard to the Original.

Art put one hand on the rounded side of the horizontal keg and made a small funnel shape over the empty tankard with his hairy, three-fingered hand. Then he began making a sound somewhere between a hum and a whistle that had a certain musical quality. For a long minute, nothing happened, but then a stream of ale began cascading into the tankard.

"That's amazing," Sue praised the Original. "I can't even imagine how useful it would be if you can do it on a larger scale."

"That's the first practical magic not involving data storage systems I've ever seen," Pffift exclaimed. "I'd be willing to reduce my commission on the supplies I'm bringing in from Eniniac if the Archmage could teach me that."

"You're just thinking you'll never have to pay for a drink again," I said. "Speaking of which, that ale is coming out of my keg even if I'm not drawing it, so it will cost you six copper."

"It was four copper the last time I was here!"

"That's before we became a café and raised our prices."

Art's humming stopped just as the foam reached the rim of the tankard, and Spot's tail thumped the floor a few times in a show of approval.

"Are your clones all progressing at the same speed?" I asked.

"You seem to forget that we're all me, just distributed over a number of bodies. We may seem to be moving in opposite directions at times, but you're really just observing different aspects of my mind coming to the fore. When we're all in close physical proximity and concentrating on the same goal, I can achieve a much higher flow rate."

"Can you do it from a distance?" Pffift asked, obviously focused on the potential for liquid larceny.

"I can't," Art replied. "You'd have to ask the Archmage what's possible. For all we know, he could be drinking out of the keg as we speak."

I looked at Spot suspiciously. Was it my imagination, or had I been filling his water bowl less often than back on Earth. Trying not to be too obvious, I lifted the new keg and made a mental note of its weight.

"Are you going to start forcing your baristas to keep a record of every tankard they draw?" Pffift asked.

Sometimes I would swear that out of all of my friends, the Hanker was the best mind-reader.

"Just making sure it's stable before I drive in the tap," I lied. "Now, where's my mallet?"

"Mind if I pour one for myself?" Art asked while I searched behind the bar.

"Knock yourself out," I told him.

Eleven

"You know," Bob said, after we all piled out of the bus. "I've been to more county fairs than you can count, but this is the first time I haven't been working the police detail."

"I can count pretty high," Monos objected, "and Naomi can count even higher because she just adds 'plus one' to whatever I say."

"You guys have counting contests?" eBeth asked her young business partners.

"Not since our first year at school," Naomi replied. "Why did you even bring that up, Monos?"

"Because he challenged me."

"It's an expression where Bob comes from," I informed the boy. "It just means he's been to a lot of county fairs."

"I've got to get going now or I'm going to start losing potential customers to the hayride," Peter called from the driver's seat of the steam-powered bus. "Don't forget you promised to bring me something good for lunch, eBeth."

"I won't—forget, I mean. See you in around four hours," she shouted back.

"Why doesn't he take a break for lunch so we can all eat together?" Sue asked.

"Paul is letting him keep half of the income from giving rides around the fair, and yesterday he made almost ten silver."

"Ten silver!" Monos exclaimed. "I want to drive the bus."

"You aren't old enough," eBeth told him. "You have to be at least sixteen."

"I've been driving my family's oxcart since I was eight, and oxen are stubborn. All Peter has to do is turn the wheel and push the lever forward when he wants it to go faster." A few hundred feet away at the pick-up point for tours, eBeth's boyfriend pulled the steam release valve, giving off a whistle that could be heard all over the fairgrounds. "Oh, and pull the rope when you want it to whistle."

"Still, how much would it cost him to take off a half an hour for lunch?" Sue persisted.

"He's saving for something," eBeth said. Then she blushed lightly and added, "I think it's for me."

"Ah, that's different then. Well, the women in my weaving circle told me there are always booths selling dress patterns, and I doubt that any of you will be interested in that, so why don't you go ahead and I'll find you later."

"I'm going to help Mark do some shopping for the café," eBeth told her young partners after Sue headed off in the direction of the home-crafting section, which stretched for a hundred booths towards the first agricultural tent. "Do you two want to stay with us or are you going to try the rides?"

"The rides," Monos answered for both of them, without hesitation.

"If you get tired and you can't find us, hop on the bus and tell Peter to give three short whistles," I told them. "We'll come and meet you. Spot, where are you going?"

The Archmage ignored me and followed the children, apparently more interested in rides than shopping.

"What sort of decorations are we looking for?" Bob asked eBeth, proving that he had correctly identified the true leader of the café shopping expedition.

"Anything old that fits in," she told him. "When Mark bought The Eatery, it didn't have many tea cups or saucers since they mainly sold local meat dishes and ale. On top of that, all of the dishes and stuff they did have matched because they bought it from a mail order supplier. Then, when Mark went back to Earth and ordered those espresso machines, he bought matching cups for them as well."

"And nobody has complained," I pointed out.

"Your cups lack character," eBeth said. "It's supposed to be a café, not a chain restaurant. Helen took me to a cool place near her college back on Earth and nothing there matched."

"She has a point," Bob concurred. "After I took over your restaurant and quit drinking, I started going to some local cafés myself. Most of the cups and plates looked like they had been bought at tag sales."

I wasn't enthusiastic about the idea of spending good coin on damaged crockery, but I knew that the baker and his extended family had bought new tableware in bulk for all of the eating places they had opened in the village, so maybe a bunch of mismatched cups and saucers would help my café stand out from the crowd. Besides, used china had to be cheaper than new. The fallacy of my logic became clear with eBeth's first purchase.

"Ten copper a cup? I can get new ones for less than half of that."

"Not like these, Mark," eBeth explained. "Just look at the gold on the handles and the rims."

"It's gilt, not real."

"Duh. And the flower pattern on this one is so pretty."

"Half of the blue blossoms are chipped off," I pointed out.

"That's what I meant by character. Let me do the shopping and you do the paying."

"Practicing for being married?" Bob asked me, as eBeth moved on to the next table and began making a pile of unmatched plates that were painted with fanciful representations of various desserts.

"Very funny." I paid the owner of the booth and waited expectantly for him to pack the cups for me. Instead, he busied himself marking prices with a grease pencil on new inventory that he drew from a seemingly endless supply under the table. "Don't I get a box with these?"

"Three copper."

"For an empty box?"

"I'll throw in some paper for wrapping cups."

I sighed and forked over three copper coins, packed my purchases, and then followed Bob on eBeth's trail of value destruction. An hour later, when we reached the end of the booths that specialized in ripping off new café owners, I was convinced that the box had been my best purchase.

"Look at that barrel," Bob said, pointing at an oversized bucket made of straight slats that didn't even touch each other. "I could have built one of those even without YouTube videos."

"It's some kind of fruit press," I deduced from the long handle screwed through the metal frame where it crossed over the top of the bucket. "You could fill it with pieces of apple, screw down the handle, and the juice comes out between the slats and runs into that tray."

"Buy it," eBeth advised.

"We have an iron juicer that fits on the counter and is good for making single drinks," I told her. "One pressing from that thing would make more juice than we sell in a week."

"I didn't mean to make juice with, Mark. It's got great visuals. I can see it in the front corner between the two small tables as a privacy screen."

"Or, we could fill the whole café with antique junk and take out all of the tables save one. That would be really private."

"Just because you've become human enough to understand sarcasm doesn't mean you should attempt it," she told me. "At least find out how much it is."

The eclectic collection of broken tools and mechanical devices displayed on the large table made me suspect that somebody had found them while cleaning out a hayloft. I reluctantly approached the woman, set down my box of mismatched china, and promised myself to bargain her down to half of the asking price.

"Does the fruit press still work?"

"Beats me," she replied. "The screw looks pretty rusted up and some of the slats don't look like they'd take the pressure if it turned, though the iron hoops holding the thing together are in decent shape."

"So, how much?" I asked.

"If you had been here the first day of the fair, the price was five silver."

"Five silver! How about the second day?"

"Four silver," she replied, and I swear the corner of her mouth twitched up.

"The third day?"

The woman held up three fingers.

"Isn't today the tenth day of the fair?" I asked.

"The last," she agreed.

"So how much is it now?"

"Ten copper. If you want to gamble on waiting to the end of the day, you can have it for free if nobody takes it. The same goes for all of this junk."

"So you really are cleaning out a hayloft." I congratulated myself on my insight.

"Cow shed, but same difference," she replied, and snuck a peek in my cardboard box. "If I had known you were coming, I would have cleaned out my kitchen cabinets as well."

"Ten copper works for me," I said, feeling that bargaining at this point would just be rude.

"You look like a strong man. You could stack all of your treasures in the tub and leave the box with me."

"I paid three copper for this box," I told her, and beckoned to Bob. "Which one of these do you want to carry?"

"The box looks cleaner."

"We should go wait on the track around the fairgrounds for Peter to come by so you can put those things in the luggage storage space under the bus," eBeth suggested.

"I don't mind carrying the press around," I said hastily, fearing that the girl wanted to clear the decks for another load. "Are you alright with the box, Bob?"

"Don't worry, Mark. I'm done for now," eBeth said. "It's better not to do all the buying for something like this in one place. There will be more fairs."

"I can't wait," I muttered.

"Hey," Bob said, stopping at a booth on our way to intercept the bus. "Isn't that one of those drawknives you said I'd need to shape real barrel staves?"

I paused to examine the collection of woodworking tools on the table the former policeman had pointed out. "Yes, but you don't need it now. The form we made up for Spot's cask is finished, I just need to pop over to Earth and pick up the right resin for the laminations. But those carving tools look like they're perfectly suited for wood-block printing."

"Getting in touch with your artistic side?"

Setting my nonfunctional juice press down in the grass, I began examining the various gouges, knives, and cutters. The brass ring on the blade of the first cutter I picked up slid easily off the handle, and removing the blade, I saw that it had only been sharpened a couple times at most. The other tools were in equally good condition, and the handles were turned from a fine grained hardwood, I believe cherry.

"You have an eye for quality craftsmanship," the booth's owner said, timing his pitch perfectly. "Those blades are hand forged by a master on one of our sister worlds and are imported specially by the woodblock printers association. If that set wasn't missing the middle knife, it would be worth three gold easy."

"Three gold?" Repeating prices to salesmen was getting to be a habit with me that I'd have to watch.

"Like I said—if," the seller reminded me. "Are you in the printing business?"

"My daughter," I said, pointed in the direction of eBeth's vanishing back. "She and her partners are running a letterpress with metal type, but they paid somebody else to prepare the woodblocks for illustrations in the one booklet that included artwork."

"And you're thinking of encouraging their artist to learn carving? It will take a while before he'll see a benefit from using the best tools," the man said slowly. "I have a beginner's set here somewhere that I could let you have for two silver…"

"The boy is a fast learner and who knows if I'll still be around to buy him a new set when the time comes."

"How about this? I'll sell you the professional set, missing the middle knife, for one gold, and I'll throw in the beginner's set for free. And they'll have to run the pages twice, you know. It will be impossible for an amateur carver to get the relief height to come out consistently the same as metal type."

"Can't we just sand or plane the back of the woodblock down after the fact until the height is correct?"

"If your eye is that good," the man said. "Take your cuts off the end grain and the blocks will hold up for thousands of impressions."

I was glad that eBeth wasn't there to see me paying a gold piece that was worth thirty-six hundred copper coins after my complaining about her purchases, and I loaded both sets of carving tools into the cider press. I'd give Monos the cheap set to practice with when we got back and set aside the good set for when I thought it would make a difference. But did that mean I had to buy Naomi something as well? I asked Bob.

"It's hard to imagine she wouldn't feel a little left out if you give her best friend a present," he told me. "You said that the boy has an artistic streak. What's her special thing?"

"She's smart, and a good student as well. She's probably the best English speaker on the planet, Earth expatriates and AI excluded," I qualified my statement.

"How about a dictionary?"

"I take it you've never read Thackeray's Vanity Fair."

"Was it published before I was born?"

"Before your grandfather was born, your great-grandfather too, most likely."

"And was it on any of my reading lists in school?" Bob continued with the interrogation.

"Probably not."

"Then I haven't read it, and neither has anybody else my age."

"I wouldn't go that far," I protested. "It's a classic."

"Do I look like I'm wearing contact lenses?"

"What does that have to do with it."

"People with glasses or contacts read classics."

"I withdraw my observation. I only meant to say that giving a dictionary to a young woman can backfire in spectacular fashion."

"How about a puppy?" Bob suggested.

"She lives at home so I'd have to clear it with the family first. I was thinking more in line with something I could buy at the fair."

"Then let's find the kids and establish surveillance. Eventually she'll slip up and show an interest in something."

"She's not a criminal, Bob," I told him, and then let the conversation drop because we had caught up with eBeth, who was waiting at the edge of the path for the slow-moving bus. To my surprise, Monos and Naomi were riding up front with Peter. I tried to ignore the fact that the boy was the one steering.

"Just a quick stop, folks," Peter promised the paying customers. He blew off the excess boiler pressure with a long whistle, set the brake, and hopped out to open the luggage compartment. Naomi forced the boy to follow before he could attempt to hijack the bus.

"Did you two get tired of the rides already?" I asked, after stowing the cider press below the bus.

"We ran out of money," Naomi explained.

"I thought eBeth gave you each twenty copper from your earnings," I said. The lion's share of the income from MeAN Publishers was earmarked for paying down the cost of the equipment, and while mail-order sales were highly profitable, they were also selling pamphlets through distribution, which demanded a deep discount and involved long delays before payment.

"I lost most of it," Monos admitted sheepishly. "Naomi wanted the stuffed bunny for her little sister and the game looked so easy. I still don't understand why I couldn't win."

"He came so close that we kept trying," Naomi spoke up in the boy's defense. "It's almost like they were cheating somehow, but it was a simple ring toss. The woman running the booth dropped the wooden ring over the post after every three throws just to show it could be done."

"That's a classic scam," Bob told us, standing a little straighter after having gotten rid of the box of china. "You bring us to the booth and I'll get your money refunded."

"I'm going to go around a few times with Peter and see the fair," eBeth announced. "Mark, advance them another twenty coppers and I'll pay you back."

Peter and eBeth climbed into the bus and he inched forward the lever that allowed steam to enter the cylinder and force the piston outwards. As soon as the bus began to move forward without breaking traction, Peter eased open the valve feeding the cylinder, and the vehicle rapidly picked up speed.

"It's this way," Monos declared, and surprised me by grabbing my hand and pulling me in the direction of the midway. The rides were much smaller than those at Earth fairs, and without amplified equipment for playing back sound recordings, the noise was limited to screaming children and a steam organ. I couldn't help doing a quick structural analysis on the wooden rollercoaster as we passed, and despite the fact that it had obviously made it through the first nine days of the fair, I wasn't crazy about the safety margins.

"There it is," Naomi told Bob, pointing at a garish booth with large stuffed animals decorating the façade. "It's four copper for three tosses, and Monos spent all that we had left after riding the roller coaster twice."

"You two stay here and leave this to the pros," Bob said. He squared his shoulders and set off for the booth, which was run by an imposing woman who I have to admit looked tougher than either my companion or myself. "What do you think, Mark. Good cop, bad cop?"

"They don't have any cops on this world, not in the Earth sense," I told him. "The cities have public safety employees and probably some detectives, but they never had an industrial revolution here and the society is a lot more stable than you'd think. There's a circuit court that can deputize locals if they need enforcement, but it rarely comes up in rural areas."

"So what's the plan?" he asked, pulling me to a stop before we got within earshot of the booth.

"I doubt she understands English, Bob, so we can talk in front of her. And my plan is to play ring toss."

"Step right up!" the barker cried the moment we made eye contact. "Three throws for four copper. Win a prize for every ring you make. Just watch me."

Standing right next to the target, she rapidly tossed three rings onto the post, though given her arm extension, dropping them straight down would be a more accurate description.

"That's the scam," Bob informed me. "The holes in those rings are just a hair wider than the post. It's almost impossible to land one while standing in front of the booth."

"I'll give it a try," I told the woman, slapping the coins down on the counter. She retrieved the three rings, carefully keeping her body out of my line of sight so I could see that I was receiving the same rings that had fit on the post.

"Make sure that the stuffed animals are the prizes," Bob advised me. "Sometimes they do a bait-and-switch and give you some trash prize that's not on display."

"I can win three of these with my three tosses?" I asked, pointing up at the stuffed animals above the counter.

"You pick 'em," she said. "I run an honest operation."

I accepted the three wooden rings she pressed into my hands, though given the size of the hole, they looked more like solid wheels for a toy wagon than hoops for a ring toss game. I held two of them in my left hand and weighed the one in my right while calculating the necessary vectors. Then I flipped it in the direction of the post in a high arc, end-over-end, and it rattled home, making a ratchet sound.

"Hey, what kind of throw was that?"

"The sign doesn't say anything about how I throw," I retorted, lining up for a second shot.

"Well, I do," the woman said, interposing herself between the counter and the post. "Either toss like a normal person or pick up your four copper and go."

"Bob, take down a bunny," I instructed my companion, and he did so with a grin. "Now, I have two more tosses," I continued, using my most authoritative voice on the proprietress. "If you object to my technique, I won't repeat it, and if you object to my presence, I'll throw both rings at the same time to get it over with. How does that suit you?"

She looked at me suspiciously, but greed won out over caution, and she said, "Throw them both at once."

I held the two rings together and cast them directly at the post with just enough angle so that when the first ring was trying to bounce off, the second ring was glancing off the top of it, causing the first ring to settle on the post and drop home. The barker gaped at the post, then turned to me angrily and said, "You cheated."

"Takes one to know one," Monos heckled her, and I realized that the children had ignored our instructions and followed us to the booth.

"Which animal do you want?" Bob asked the boy.

"I'm too old for stuffed animals, but Naomi has two little sisters, so maybe another bunny."

"Make it a cow," she said. "Sarah is at the cow age."

After my ring-toss heroics, I could do no wrong in the eyes of the kids. Rather than going on more rides, they elected to stay with us as I homed in on Sue's location transponder to make sure she wasn't spending me into the poor house. We reached her just as she was leaving a cabinet-maker's booth with a large wooden chest.

"Here, let me carry that," I said. Even though we were no longer undercover, it wouldn't accomplish anything for my second-in-command to show off her super-human strength. "Is this full of patterns?"

"Half-full," she admitted.

"You couldn't get a cardboard box?"

"It's furniture," Monos informed me. "It goes at the foot of your bed."

"It's a hope chest," Sue said, adding for the benefit of the children who thought we were already husband and wife, "I didn't have one before we got married so I'm playing catch-up."

135

Twelve

"Hurry up or we'll be late to the first official town meeting," Sue said impatiently.

"It's this necktie," I complained, undoing the knot and starting over again. "I think it's defective."

"I told you to tack one of eBeth's instruction sheets on the wall," she said, stepping forward and taking up the ends of the tie. I dropped my hands to my sides in relief. "Is your memory giving you problems again? Have you been keeping an eye on your magic emanations dosimeter?"

"I remember the instructions perfectly well, and I helped Monos when he carved the woodblocks for printing. It's just different somehow when I'm in a hurry and you're in the room."

My second-in-command completed the knot before I finished speaking, snugged and straightened the tie, then stepped back to observe her work.

"Your shoes are almost too shiny," she said. "The villagers are going to think you're trying to show them up."

"Townspeople now, not villagers," I reminded her, "and I hope they know me better than that. We better get moving. The Ferrymen's temple is probably going to be packed."

"Are Delilah and Athena watching the café?" Sue asked as we headed downstairs.

"I told them to close during the meeting so they could attend. This is a big deal for Covered Bridge, changing from a village to a town. It's a story they can tell their children."

"Maybe," she said doubtfully as we exited out the front and started for the temple. "None of the women in my weaving circle seemed very excited about it."

"I just hope the council of elders doesn't blame us for forcing the change," I said. "I didn't even realize that Kim and Justin had over a hundred people working in their mail-order operation until I asked them about it yesterday. It's no wonder Paul has to send the bus farther and farther from town to find lodging for his workers."

"We may have been the catalyst, but some of the growth in town has little to do with us, at least not directly." Sue looked back over her shoulder and frowned. "I wonder why there aren't more people out walking to the Ferrymen's temple for the meeting?"

"Because we're late," I surmised. "Bob is going with Lilith, it's sort of their first date, and Pffift had some things to do out at his warehouse, but he said he would ride in with Hosea because he's interested in how humans govern themselves. I hope eBeth and Peter show up. They're both old enough to vote if they were back on Earth."

"Isn't that Saul entering the temple? Do you think he came in for the meeting?"

"That did look like his bald spot. He owns a place on the lake so that makes him a resident. If the meeting's already begun and there aren't any seats available in the back, let's just stand rather than making people move for us."

"I'm beginning to think that you may be the most excited sentient in town," Sue said with a laugh. "I hope you

137

aren't disappointed if our friends and neighbors don't share your sense of drama."

I picked up the pace without replying, and two minutes later we reached the Ferrymen's temple at the top of the hill. I could hear a number of loud conversations going on within. I hesitated at the doors after hearing my name bandied about in the general noise, but Sue took a hold of my arm and dragged me inside. The hubbub died as abruptly as a snuffed candle.

"Would everybody please take a seat so we can begin?" Palti requested from the small stage at the front of the room. Sue and I hurried past the indoor garden and had no problem finding seats together in the back row, since the hall wasn't even at a quarter of its capacity. "We all know each other, and I haven't quite finished reading through the new rulebook for town meetings that the county commissioner sent me, so we'll proceed as we always have. I see a hand."

"Johan, ma'am. I've never been to a meeting here."

"So I was wrong about all of us knowing one another. I take it from your mismatched forearms that you must be one of the employees at the boiler-works who swings a hammer all day long. And my name is Palti, we don't stand on formalities at meetings."

"I'm a foreman at the boiler-works, and my co-workers asked me to come and represent them."

"I'm Dvora, and the pickers and packers at the Healing Herbs distribution center delegated me to speak for them," a small woman sitting next to Johan spoke up.

"Excellent, glad to have you both here," Palti said. "Everybody who lives in our community is welcome to participate, and I'll give you a quick rundown on how we operate. In the past, we held a lottery every year at the

138

Ferrymen's Day festival to choose a secretary for meetings. I drew the short straw the last time around. But the recently completed county census determined that we now have the population to incorporate as a town, and the council of elders put in the paperwork, which has already been accepted."

"Why did they do that?" somebody moaned loudly.

"Moving to an executive form of government means that the elders won't be constantly bombarded with complaints about cows getting loose and smoky chimneys, Hosea. If you're interested in standing—"

"Not me," the farmer hastily interrupted. "I was just curious."

"Very well," Palti said, looking over the crowd to see if there were any other dissenters. "We all know that the rapid changes in this town are due to the presence of Mark and his team, so before we continue, I'd like to invite him to come up here and answer any questions you may have. Mark?"

I pointed my finger at my own chest to make sure she was in fact calling me out and it wasn't some sort of glitch. The people in the room actually gave a little cheer when I stood up, and there was a brief chant of, "Mark, Mark, Mark." I made my way to the front of the room and stood beside the so-called Ferryman's Body, a battery-powered video editing station and projector. Artisans all over Reservation used the alien equipment to practice their self-documentary skills for producing authenticity videos to accompany exports of hand-crafted goods.

"Thank you, Palti," I said to the miller's wife, before turning to address the assembly. "As you all know by now, my team members and I are not from this world, and with the exception of eBeth and Peter, we aren't even human.

139

That said, we are bound by the rules of our League and we try to act in accordance with your best interests."

"What's that thing around your neck?" Sophus asked from the crowd.

"My necktie? I'm sure you must have seen them when you took our Earth tour."

A number of attendees who had been on one of our package tours either shook their heads in denial or spoke up to say that they didn't recall. Then several of the women commented that the tie made me look quite debonair, and Pffift took the opportunity to stand up and make a few quick sales. I noticed that the energy in the room seemed to be picking up a notch, and I felt vindicated in my claim to Sue that the meeting would be one which attendees would recount to their children.

"I don't have a prepared speech," I continued, "so unless you want to hear the pitch I made for Earth to join the League, I'll just say that I'm happy to take any questions, and the door to my café is always open."

"I have a question about the housing shortage," Xeres announced.

"Before you ask, let me thank all of you who have provided a temporary home to the students in our night school for Earth tourism," I said. "If my team members were here tonight, I'm sure that they would also express their gratitude to everybody for chipping in and providing room and board for their workers. I'm encouraged to see some new boarding houses going up across from Paul's boiler-works, and I'm sure it's only a matter of time before you're relieved of the burden."

"That's just it," Xeres said. "I don't want to be relieved of the burden. I just want your assurances that if I add another five bedrooms to the back of my house you won't pull the rug out from under me by building a dormitory."

"You're lucky that your farm is so close to town," Yitzhak complained. "Hosea and I have too many rooms, but we only get the overflow if everybody closer to town runs out of space, and that's only possible if Paul sends the kid around with the steam bus. What we need to grow this town is regular bus service."

"It does seem a shame to have a bus sitting next to the boiler-works doing nothing all day," Hosea added so quickly that I was suspicious the two farmers had coordinated beforehand.

"I'd be willing to build a little shed beside the road with a bench and a sign so that everybody near my farm could wait there," Yitzhak added.

"You mean a bus stop sign?" I asked.

"With a timetable," he affirmed.

"I'll bring it up with Paul. It's his bus." I saw Delilah's aunt raise her hand and pointed at her. "Yes, Lilith?"

"When are you going to start bringing tour groups from Earth in our direction?"

"Hear, hear," a number of townspeople cried out.

"You want to be mobbed by tourists?" I asked in surprise. A quick scan of the crowd told me that Sue had been correct earlier when she spotted Saul. "Perhaps we can get a clarification from a member of the planetary administration. I thought that one of the reasons you weren't interested in joining the League was the fear of being overrun by aliens, Saul."

"There's a difference between the small tour groups you've been organizing and an invasion," the president of the Council of Spaceports replied. "And tourists from Earth aren't exactly aliens."

141

"That makes it worse," I explained. "You know that Kim does a health screen on all of your people before we agree to take them to Earth. That's to protect Earthlings from any pathogens which might have developed on this world for which humans on Earth have no immunity. Then our portal filter does a molecular-level screen when we take you there and uses that baseline to eliminate any bacteria or viruses you pick up during your trip. Aliens are much safer as tourists as you're highly unlikely to share any microscopic bugs."

"You can't do the same thing going the other direction?"

"Theoretically, yes, but the main problem is that we're using an official portal for unofficial business. Nobody on Reservation is going to complain, but people on Earth are funny that way."

"Why not ask your superiors for a waiver?" Lilith suggested. "Everybody here would be happy to sign a petition."

"And maybe you could bend the rules a little so the Earthlings could buy more stuff to bring home," said the owner of one of the faux-antique shops that had recently sprung up. Now I was beginning to see what this was all about.

"I'll ask next time I get the chance, but I have to warn you that my request will likely be denied," I told them.

The large doors at the back of the room swung open and eBeth entered with Peter. "Sorry we're late," she said, after all heads swiveled in their direction. "I warned my night class ahead of time that I'd be stepping out, but I couldn't just flee while they had questions about the material."

"Where do you stand on bringing tourists here from Earth?" Lilith asked her.

"I hadn't really thought about it," eBeth said, taking a seat next to Sue. "As long as they're polite, I guess."

"Some of them will probably try to stay," Peter contributed. "This world is a lot nicer than most places on Earth once you get used to not having Internet access."

Nobody seemed inclined to argue the point, and Palti stepped forward and asked, "Does anybody else have a question for Mark?"

"I do," the baker said, rising to his feet. "I know that you and your team have done a lot for this town and for Reservation as a whole, and I especially appreciate the custom culinary tour that Sue and Stacey arranged for my family. But we're also competitors, and if you're going to bring Earth technology through your portal to use in your café, I think the local business community should be allowed to do the same."

"Are you talking about my espresso machine?" I asked. "We only use it when it gets busy."

"Sit down," the baker's wife hissed, pulling on his arm. "You're embarrassing me."

"I have a question," Athena said, rising to her feet. "When is Helen coming back, and can you get her to open a pole-dancing school in town now that we're growing so fast?"

"I anticipate her return any day, but she'll be filling in at our tourism office and the café's kitchen while Sue is away," I replied.

"If my daughter is going to study pole-dancing, I don't feel so guilty about this," Palti muttered to me as she stepped forward again.

I knew that she worried about Helen's influence on Athena, but I couldn't see where I fit in, unless she was going to publicly forbid her daughter from working in my café.

"Are there any other candidates?" Palti asked the gathered townspeople. I didn't have a clue what she was talking about, but I didn't like the sound of that 'other.' Everybody else in the room froze as if they were at an art auction and frightened that an inadvertent muscle twitch could be interpreted as a positive response. "Then I nominate Mark to be the first mayor of Covered Bridge."

"Second the nomination," Hosea called out before I could react.

"Third," Pffift cried.

"Your vote doesn't count," I shouted at the Hanker. "You don't even live here."

"I'm renting from Hosea," he reminded me.

"I'm willing to accept the third," Palti said. "In accordance with Section Three, Subparagraph Two of the law for special elections by town meeting, I call for a show of hands on the candidate. Everybody who supports Mark for mayor?"

I swear every hand in the room but mine went up, including the baker's.

"The motion carries. I've been asked by the Council of Elders to inform our new mayor that in the interest of a smooth transition, they will be available for consultation on request, with the stipulation that refreshments are provided and said request is made no more than once a month. Does anybody have any questions?"

"Me," I said, poking Palti in the shoulder to get her to look in my direction. "How can you make an artificial intelligence construct from another world your mayor?"

"Through the legal process of a town meeting nomination and a show of hands," she replied calmly. "I may not

144

have read the entire rulebook, but I'm confident that it won't contain anything prohibiting alien AI from standing for office."

"That's because they couldn't imagine anybody would ever nominate somebody like me," I protested.

"If there's no further business, this meeting is adjourned," Palti called out loudly, and there was a stampede for the doors.

I was so taken off-guard that I didn't protest further, and Sue reached me a minute later, her eyes shining with something more than infrared signaling. "I'm so proud of you," she said. "Mayor of Covered Bridge. Who would believe it?"

"Way to go, Mark," eBeth chipped in. "Spot's going to be sorry he missed the meeting."

"Congratulations, Mr. Ai," Peter said. "I'd be honored to buy you an ale. I've never known a mayor before."

The thought of somebody else paying for the drinks in my café took a little of the sting out of my sneak election, and I allowed Sue to take my arm and lead me out of the Ferrymen's temple. I could tell from the posture of her human encounter suit that she really was proud of me, and I made up my mind not to let her down.

"You should get a sign for the café saying that the mayor is in or out," eBeth suggested. "It will probably be good for business. I'll bet Monos will carve it for you without even charging. And you," she said, poking her boyfriend. "Give him the message."

"Right. Paul wanted me to tell you that better you than him."

"Paul was a candidate for mayor too?" I asked, feeling slightly let down.

"We only found out right before the meeting," Peter said. "The townspeople have been preparing for this in secret, and they ended up with you, Paul, and Kim for candidates."

"I wondered where the rest of my team members were hiding," I groused. "I'll bet there's a rule against nominating candidates who aren't present at the meeting."

"Sophus did mention something about that when he stopped in the shop this afternoon to pick up a repaired gear for his mill. Somehow Paul figured out the miller was hiding something and bribed him into spilling the beans. Then he tipped off Justin and Kim, but he made me swear not to say anything to you or eBeth until after the meeting."

"Why wasn't Sue on the candidate list?" I asked, feeling indignant that she'd been left out. "Or Helen, or Stacey for that matter."

"The women in Sue's weaving circle already knew that she's leaving for the rest of the summer, so that ruled her out, and with the tourism business, Stacey is gone three weeks out of four."

"And Palti can't forgive Helen for bringing pole-dancing to Reservation," eBeth added.

"Looks like there's a little line of people in front of the café waiting to congratulate you," Sue pointed out as we approached my building.

"If they really want to make me happy, they should go in and buy something," I responded automatically, though I actually was quite touched. "I guess being popular isn't the worst thing in the world."

"Mr. Mayor," the woman who owned the general store greeted me formally. "Congratulations on your election."

"I didn't see you at the town hall meeting, Desponia," I scolded her playfully. "Good government depends on the participation of the population."

"I wanted to make sure I was first in line here," she said. "I have a complaint about the streetlights."

"But there aren't any streetlights."

"Exactly. I could understand when we were just a village and we didn't have a budget for such luxuries, but now that we're a growing town I think that streetlights on Main Street should be the top priority."

"Paving stones," said the baker's son from behind her. "Every time it rains I spend half of my day mopping the floor in my restaurant to get rid of the mud people track in."

"That's why we should have sidewalks," somebody else spoke up. "It's all well and fine for owners of buildings with a veranda to connect their frontage into a continual wooden walk, but how about those of us with stores on the other side of the road?"

"I'm all in favor of streetlights, paving, and sidewalks myself, but I've only been mayor for ten minutes and I don't know if there's room in the budget," I told them. "I don't even know if there is a budget. Why don't you all come in and we can discuss this?"

"Mark's throwing a victory party," Desponia announced. "Drinks are on the house."

Between the cheering and the handshakes, I realized I was trapped, but I made a note to myself to have Monos carve two signs. The first sign to inform people that the mayor was in or out, as eBeth had suggested, and the second stating a one-drink minimum for all visitors, no exceptions.

Thirteen

"I really appreciate your coming along," I thanked Pffift and Art as we climbed the stairs to the portal. "The head librarian can be a bit intimidating at times, but she'll be impressed that I brought you guys to the beta test."

"Is Library's visitor center really far enough along to call it a beta test?" Pffift asked. "I thought you said they just got around to adding a section with atmospheric controls."

"It did take longer than I would have expected," I replied while opening the door to the second floor closet. "The engineers always preferred maintaining a vacuum on Library because it eliminates the corrosion and dust issues that most machine-based AI would rather do without. There is no natural oxygen on Library, so they needed to import it."

"Couldn't it be processed from water or mineral oxides in the small quantities required?"

"There is no water on Library," I told Pffift. "It was a lifeless ball of rock when the first artificial intelligence arrived, and our version of terraforming was to keep it a lifeless ball of rock, but with a good power plant."

"Sounds a bit like our second homeworld," Art said nostalgically, and gestured at the portal. "After you, Pffift."

An instant later, the three of us found ourselves at the center of a cavernous metal room, bare of any furnishings. The only decoration was a giant piece of art that took the form of a circle colored by words from what I estimated were at least ten thousand distinct languages. A voice intoned, "Gerffel dimple."

"Gerffel dimple?" Pffift repeated. "What's that supposed to mean?"

"Thank you. Language identified as English. Welcome to Library's visitor center."

"May I ask to whom I am speaking?" the Hanker inquired, proving himself a veteran of many first-contact situations. "And why did you gerffel dimple us when we arrived? It sounds like a curse."

"I am the head librarian and I will be hosting all guests to the visitor center during our beta testing trials. You responded properly to my query, so I assumed you understood GUT."

"I didn't have a clue what you were saying," Pffift replied without the slightest hesitation.

"Galactic Universal Tongue," I reminded him. "Gerffel dimple is a request for a speech sample for analysis and matching. Don't they teach GUT in the schools anymore?"

"Not in Hanker schools, and I've never even heard of it. Is it a mishmash of League languages?"

"GUT predates the League by many galactic rotations," the head librarian informed us, slipping into her lecture mode. "It is the contribution of a species from the Small Magellanic Cloud that went extinct shortly after they began continually transmitting a message of brotherly peace and love across the Milky Way. In addition to proposing a universal spoken language for all sentients, they broadcast instructions for reaching their star system, not having worked out interstellar travel themselves."

"I remember how this ends," Art interjected.

"Unfortunately, the power and frequency hopping of their transmission disrupted some forms of communications systems and irritated a number of advanced species who didn't like being told how to live. Other than a recording of the actual transmission loop, my historical records of the period are sketchy. Rumor has it that a less tolerant species which had developed interstellar travel got sick of the noise and paid a visit to the Small Magellanic Cloud."

"Ancient history," Pffift concluded. "What's with the big circle thing? I've seen better abstract art on bathroom walls."

"It's a map," the head librarian informed him, and I could almost detect a note of disappointment over the Hanker's failure to identify it. "We all thought that the meaning was clear."

"Hang on a second," I said, and took another look at the giant circle. This time I began picking out and translating the phrases I recognized, all of which read, 'You are here.'"

"You are here?" Pffift asked in disbelief after I translated for him. "That's the whole map?"

"It's as far as we've gotten," the head librarian admitted. "By the time we accounted for all of the known extant languages from species that might pay us a visit, the choice was either to create a very large map or to use very small fonts. This was the compromise."

"Why would you want a printed map?" the Hanker demanded. "Do it with interactive displays or holograms and change languages on demand."

"Mark told us that all visitor centers have printed maps."

"I told you that all visitor centers on *Earth* have printed maps," I defended myself. "The portal system visitor centers that the Originals built usually have three-dimensional models of the surrounding area."

"We found that they worked best for species without printed languages," Art spoke through his pendant. "Of course, it means that the landscaping around the visitor center has to be maintained or the map goes out of date."

"Can't you create a hologram on the fly to show us the rest of your visitor center?" Pffift asked the head librarian.

"I could, but it would look just like the current map without the text."

"This is it?" I took a second look around the empty room to see if I had missed anything. "I thought we were standing in a reception hall. You haven't built anything else?"

"The engineers wanted to get some feedback from potential visitors before proceeding. I have a list of questions to ask."

"Is this really all about your wanting to meet Art?" I asked suspiciously.

"I was hoping you would invite him," the head librarian hedged. "We didn't have a suitable atmosphere before, and I could hardly ask him to come in an environmental suit and upload his mind to our infrastructure. I don't even know if we have compatible systems."

"Transferring consciousness in and out of a biological host is somewhat involved and rather time-consuming," Art told us. "We're hoping that magic will eventually help us overcome that obstacle, but none of us have actually tried leaving our host bodies since occupying them. Our telepathic connections are fast enough that I'm able to share partial back-ups with other parts of my mind when we're in close proximity, but each body has limited storage capacity, so we try to avoid more duplication than is absolutely necessary."

"That's fascinating," the head librarian said. "Do you mind if I ask—"

"—if you'd like a place to sit or something to drink?" Pffift interrupted. "How about we finish one topic before you start playing 'A Million Questions' with your new AI friend."

I stared in horror at the Hanker, expecting the head librarian to vent the atmosphere from the room or obliterate him with a static discharge, but no, she couldn't do that without injuring Art. Instead, she affected a dry chuckle which sounded a bit sinister to my paranoid ear, and said, "You are correct, of course. It's been so long since we've had guests of any sort on Library that I've forgotten my manners."

"And your furniture," Pffift observed.

"I'm afraid there's none prepared, but we do have a small supply of water for humidifying the air. I'm sure Mark's encounter suit is capable of extracting moisture from the atmosphere and condensing it into the holding tank that allows him to pretend to eat and drink."

"I'm not drinking out of one of Mark's holding tanks, thank you very much. I don't want to be a party pooper, but since I'm already here, why don't I give you my impressions? Then I'll return to Reservation and you can all talk about me behind my back."

"I have no objection," the head librarian replied stiffly. "Your unsolicited feedback is appreciated."

"First, this whole place is too shiny. I don't know if it's stainless steel or some other alloy, but a little paint would go a long way to making it feel a lot warmer."

"He's got a point," Art said. "Some sort of floor covering would be good as well. I'm not wearing shoes, and it hurts my feet just walking on this surface."

"Second, you need to break up this huge space, and I don't just mean some furniture or a better map. The perfect hemispherical roof is almost painful to look at. Build a knee wall with doors around the circumference and you can use it for storage space."

"What does a visitor center need with storage space?" the head librarian inquired icily.

"It would make a handy place to keep furniture for the various species," Pffift shot back. "Third, the lighting is horrible. How about some windows so visitors can see what it's like on Library? Is there a sun out there or are we on a rogue planet floating between stars?"

"Don't say 'rogue,'" I hissed at him. "It has a particular connotation with AI."

"This dome is on the surface," the head librarian acknowledged. "Windows are an easy engineering change order, though there isn't much to see."

"Let your visitors make that judgment for themselves," Pffift said. "If nothing else, they'll have a view of the landing field."

"Landing field?"

"Sure. Do you think I came along just to give you my opinions on interior decorating? I want to offer my services in establishing a passenger route, and it's traditional to have a fixed place to land. The visitor center can double as the terminal."

"But the portal…" I began to protest.

"Weren't you listening back on Reservation when Saul was complaining about how they couldn't get in touch with Library before you came to spy on them?" Pffift cut me off. "They aren't League members so they have no access to the portal system. And none of the League members even know where this planet is, if we're even on a planet."

"Is that accurate?" Art asked.

"Keeping our location secret seemed like a reasonable security precaution," the head librarian admitted. "There are a number of advanced species who see AI as an abomination."

"But surely you have means of defending yourselves," Art said. "I may be vulnerable to unexpected attacks in the biological form I've assumed, but the ship-construct I occupied for most of my existence could have held its own against any combination of civilizations in the galaxy."

"We may have erred on the side of caution, but as there was no immediate need to change our policy, we've kept it in place."

"And you wonder why so many of the League's members don't trust you," Pffift scolded. "The way they see it, you can hit them, but they can't hit you back."

"We would never hit them," I protested, "but if we did and they tried to hit us back, they could only do themselves harm."

"Your friend in the vat-grown body has a valid argument," the head librarian told me. "We haven't been looking at this from the standpoint of the other species. If we're going to continue with this visitor center and make it possible for non-AI to come here, we need to reexamine our tendency towards secrecy."

"But you should proceed cautiously," the Hanker added unexpectedly. "If you simply publish the location of Library, you'll be overrun by tourists and salesmen, like the rest of the League. That's why I'm offering you an exclusive passenger service, with knowledge of the actual location of Library limited to myself." He paused and amended his offer. "Well, I don't really handle navigation anymore so we'll have to let a couple of my close family members in on the deal, but if you want to install an automated system on the bridge of my ship, I'd even be willing to fly here blind."

"In return for?" I asked, having learned a thing or two about negotiating with Pffift.

"All I ask is a limited lifetime monopoly. What with the triangle trade between Earth, Eniniac and the Reservation worlds, we cover a lot of space, and that doesn't even count the distribution routes I'm running. All you'd have to do is announce that in addition to portal system access, Library can be reached by passenger service with semi-annual pickups at one or two locations. If you stick with Eniniac and Earth, I won't even charge a service fee."

"You'll bring them here for free?" the head librarian asked.

"I meant I won't charge you a fee for establishing the route," Pffift said, hugging himself with glee. "The passengers will pay what it's worth to them."

"I'll discuss your offer with our board of trustees and our representative to the League," the head librarian said, surprising me yet again. "Is there anything else you'd like to contribute?"

"You need a directory, and a messaging service."

"I don't understand."

"I lost touch with Mark for hundreds of years and I couldn't even drop him a line," Pffift said. "Was I supposed to approach Library-affiliated AI at random asking if they knew him? That's like some alien approaching me and saying, 'Oh, you're a Hanker. Do you know Brivel?'"

"Brivel?" I asked.

"It's the most common baby name the last hundred years or so, both sexes. My point is, I couldn't even send you a postcard to ask how you were doing."

"And you really wanted to get in touch with me?"

"Mark, don't take this the wrong way, but as far as artificial intelligences go, you're a wrecking ball. I'm a businessman and I thrive on creative destruction. How many new deals have I made since catching up with you on Earth less than two years ago?"

"Several," I said, unsure how I felt about the Hanker's characterization of my personality.

"Plus, you're a fun guy, and one of the best friends I've ever had," Pffift added. "Now this place really does hurt my eyes, so open the portal and I'll see you back in your café. I'm going to pick up a pizza."

I sent my friend on his way and prepared myself for the wrath of the head librarian, but she was far more interested in talking with Art than nursing any grudges against the plainspoken Hanker.

"I understand that you're able to generate a weak radio frequency carrier through purely biological processes," the head librarian addressed the Original.

"Yes, I used to communicate with Mark that way, but it takes more energy than telepathy. We guided the evolution of the species from which we clone bodies to create a general purpose biological platform."

"But you can't even speak intelligibly without that pendant," I said. "And don't call that fax machine noise you make speech. Spot is probably the only non-AI in the League who can make sense of it."

"Telepathy is a lesser form of magic," Art explained. "It's akin to empathy and arises naturally in some species, but telepaths who can communicate with alien species are rare. I can't explain to you how my telepathy-to-speech pendant works because it is a magical rather than a technological device, and I have a long way to go before I reach that level of arcane knowledge."

"I'm sure you've heard this all before, Mark, and it can't be very interesting to you," the head librarian insinuated. "Why don't you head back and I'll send Art along when we're done talking? I'm sure you must have mayoral duties to attend."

There was no mistaking the underlying order in her question, so I told Art that I'd wait for him in the café, and returned to Reservation. Stepping out of the second-floor closet, I almost ran into eBeth, who immediately began trying to renegotiate the deal we'd made for MeAN Publishers to print 14,400 illustrated instruction sheets for tying a necktie.

"I timed Monos operating the press with Naomi helping to pump the foot pedal, and at best they can do four sheets a minute."

"Bob can do ten sheets a minute," I told her. "You should hire him."

"Alright, say ten sheets a minute, but with time out for inking and paper resupply, that's only five hundred copies an hour."

"So it's a twenty-nine hour job. What's the problem?"

"You're not paying us enough to buy the paper, the ink, and to hire Bob to run the letterpress all week, if he'll even do it. And I'm not even counting the time Monos spent carving the woodblock illustrations."

"He's really good, isn't he?" I said, escaping onto the stairway. "If I had known that he learned carving at home, I would have started him with the professional tools."

"His family does fancy woodcarving on millwork for export to other worlds," eBeth replied, keeping right on my heels. "This is our first contract job and I don't want the kids to get disappointed and quit."

"Then why did you agree to Pffift's offer?"

"Because he's a better businessman than I am," eBeth said bluntly. "He should be, given the fact he's been running a galactic trading business for hundreds of years. Which of you is older?"

"Pffift," I said. "Hankers grow themselves new bodies on a regular basis and their brains hold up for a few thousand years. How much more do you need?"

"The current deal covers the cost of materials plus fifty copper," she said. "I figured we owe you since you don't charge us to work in the café, but our profit comes to less than two copper an hour. Since you raised the prices, Bob would have to work three hours just to buy an ale."

"He doesn't drink alcohol," I observed, walking out the front door and into the street. "Give me an amount and I'll talk to Pffift."

"I was thinking of something else," eBeth said, and the change in her voice made me turn around and look at her. "We're printing the instructions on one side."

"You want to change the layout and print on both sides? But that will double the amount of time it takes. You'll save half of the paper, but that can't come to more than a handful of copper coins."

"We don't want to save paper, Mark. I had an offer to print an advertisement on the other side."

"For what?"

"Kim and Justin's mail-order business. Actually, Paul is interested in printing some advertisements as well, but he said that neckties and machine shops don't mix. And Sue wants to promote the travel business, but we agreed on a separate deal to include those ads in our English pamphlets."

"Are you going to tell me how much Kim and Justin offered you to print their ad on the back of the necktie instruction sheets?"

"Enough to pay Bob or somebody else to run the press," she replied evasively. "I'm trying to learn how to delegate."

"Go ahead and print the ads," I told her, making the decision for Pffift as well as myself. If he complained, I'd just point out that the girl was following his advice better than I ever could. "But I want Bob, or whoever you hire, to do most of the printing in the morning. I'm as big a fan of ambiance as the next person, but with that heavy flywheel keeping the press running smoothly, it's dangerous to operate if we get crowded."

"You know that these people all grew up on farms, Mark. They have more sense than to stick their hands into moving machinery."

"How many butchers do you know who still have all of their fingers?" I asked her.

"Well, none, but I don't actually know any butchers."

"I helped set up a point-of-sale system for a specialty meats shop back on Earth. There were three butchers working there, and all of them were down at least a fingertip. Accidents happen even to the most experienced people, which is why Paul told you that neckties and machine shops don't mix. And when you and Peter get married, don't be surprised if he leaves his wedding ring home when he goes to work. Rings and machine shops don't mix either."

"You're right," she conceded. "I just wanted to finish the job quickly, but if you guys aren't in a rush, we can take a couple of weeks."

"Pffift is going to a fashion tradeshow in the provincial capital next week to look for retailers. He'll bring a few dozen samples with him, but we're primarily focused on selling in bulk."

"Are you planning on making a regular business of it?" eBeth asked, obviously thinking ahead to future advertising sales.

"Without patent protection, you know that every clothes maker on Reservation will bring their own neckties to market if they catch on," I told her.

"Where are you going now?"

"The baker's. Pffift is getting pizza and I need to remind him that we've changed to a vegetarian kitchen."

Fourteen

"What do you think?" Bob asked the Archmage.

Spot stood in front of the full-length mirror in eBeth's bedroom and turned his head from side to side, admiring the faux-brandy cask he was wearing around his neck. Then he broke into a big doggy smile and took off down the stairs and out the front door, no doubt to show off the new look to his friends.

"You did a good job, Bob," I told the former policeman. "It couldn't have weighed much more than a large apple."

"That's because he hasn't filled it yet. I wonder if he'll use the telekinetic trick you said that Art did with the beer. Speaking of which, when do I get paid?"

"I'm sure Spot will tell the Originals, and then Art will dig up some gold from wherever they keep it stashed and bring it to you. Are you going to spend it taking a trip around Reservation? Sue knows a number of travel agents."

"Why should I go anywhere when I have a free place to stay, a date with Lilith this Friday, and my job working for eBeth? Don't tell her I said this, but I actually like running that treadle-powered letterpress," Bob confessed, and in an impressive display of coordination, he balanced on one foot while pumping the other leg, as if he was operating the printing press. "If I wasn't retired, I'd be tempted to set up a little printing business of my own."

"You're not even forty-five yet and you've been working harder the last few weeks than any time since I've known you. Why do you keep on talking about being retired?"

"So I don't forget and do something stupid like start a new career. I better get downstairs and spin up the flywheel so I can finish printing ads on the back of your instruction sheets for the ties. Did I tell you that I'm almost up to twenty sheets a minute? That's faster than Art."

"You've definitely got skills," I congratulated him. "Don't forget that everybody has to stay behind the rope barrier while you're working."

"Where did you even find those red velvet ropes with the brass ends and stanchions?" Bob asked. "I feel like I'm playing piano in a luxury hotel, but nobody can get close enough to put money in the tip jar."

"That's because I bought the ropes and stanchions from a luxury hotel. I'll see you in a few minutes."

After Bob headed downstairs to his part-time printing job, I slipped into the master bedroom to snoop around in private. Sue was up to something, and I was afraid that if I let it come as a surprise I'd react the wrong way and hurt her feelings. I examined her hope chest across the full spectrum to make sure she hadn't set any alarms, and then eased open the lid. There wasn't anything new since the last time I had checked, just a stack of patterns that she'd bought at the fair and a few partially completed outfits.

"Mark?" eBeth called from the bottom of the steps, making me jump half out of my shoes. I quickly closed the lid and hastened to the landing.

"What's up?" I asked in my most casual tone.

She gave me a suspicious look. "Why are you acting guilty?"

"I'm not acting guilty," I protested, and made a show of clomping down the stairs like an AI without a care in the world. "Why did you call me?"

"Paul is coming over to get a quote for some booklets. It's a big job, so I was hoping you'd sit in and give me some pointers."

"I take it Pffift isn't back from the tradeshow yet."

"I would have asked you even if he was," she said, but I could tell from the slight shift of the tendons under the skin of her neck that she was crossing her fingers behind her back. Then she held up her hand to stop me from entering the café, and added, "Try not to act weird when the kids thank you for your gifts."

I suspected she was just changing the subject, but I had to ask anyway. "What do you mean, weird?"

"You know, like joking that they can pay you back by doing chores around the café for the next four years."

"It never even occurred to me," I lied, disappointed to hear that nobody appreciated my sense of humor. "Are you sure that Naomi's parents aren't angry about the pony? It's a big responsibility, and they eat quite a bit."

"Nobody gets mad about being given a free pony, at least, not on Reservation," she told me. "I just hope that Naomi doesn't spend so much time riding and taking care of it that she neglects her schoolwork."

"I hadn't thought about that part. It would be a shame if she quit your business when you have all this work coming in."

"That won't be an issue, Mark. There's plenty of time in the day, it's just a matter of how kids want to spend it. Working and making money like an adult is a huge attraction, but you give a girl her age a choice between ponies and algebra homework? I know which one I would have chosen."

"You grew up in an apartment in a public housing project and I'll bet you never saw a pony in real life before we came here."

"What difference does that make? Anyway, how did you even know she was saving to buy Yitzhak's pony?"

"I have my sources," I said, trying to sound mysterious.

"So you had Bob investigate her," eBeth surmised.

I stood on my right to remain silent and followed her into the café. It was mid-afternoon and the large dining room was at full capacity. In addition to a section of the tables inside, Athena was handling the overflow seated at the picnic benches in the backyard, which she had dubbed 'The Garden Room', while Delilah frequently stuck her head out the front door to check if the customers at the two small tables on the veranda needed anything. It was good business was booming because that trained pony cost even more than the professional-grade woodblock engraver's tools I'd bought for Monos.

"It's fortunate I finished processing that last batch of tourists early because you're seriously short on help," Sue said to me as I slipped in behind the bar to take over. "At least we're getting some use out of the big espresso machine."

"Thanks for filling in. I've been trying to find help, but between Kim and Justin hiring for their mail-order operation and Paul adding more manufacturing space to his business practically every day, there's just nobody left in the area who wants to wait tables or make drinks."

"You might raise the wages," Sue suggested. "Kim pays a silver a day with free medical benefits, and Paul pays ten silver a week, plus profit sharing."

164

"Providing medical help is a bonus for Kim, it's what she likes doing, and working for Paul is like working for an Internet start-up back on Earth. He gets the employees so excited that they're all putting in eighty and ninety hours a week. Besides, my employees get tips, and when it's this busy, I'll bet the waitresses are tripling their base pay."

"Stacey can fill in for me running the office between taking tour groups to Earth, but I'm going to be away until the end of the summer. I'm not sure you realize how much time I spend baking for the café and filling in when you're short-handed."

I almost asked her if her trip was really that important but caught myself at the last second. I'd gone a couple hundred years without seeing Sue more than a handful of times before she had herself assigned to my Observer team on Earth. If the number of loose ends I'd left dangling around the galaxy during that period were any guide, I'm sure she had some cleanup of her own to do.

"Are you sure you don't need any money?" I asked her. "At least let me give you the code for my Library account in case you get back there and find yourself short."

"I'll be fine, Mark, and I'm sure I have more in my Library account than you and the rest of the team combined. I know you're only marrying me for my wealth."

"That's not—" I began to protest before I realized she was laughing at me. How eBeth could accuse me of having a weird sense of humor while not saying anything about Sue and her marriage jokes was beyond me. I made a show of checking the order slates to regain my dignity, and started on a cappuccino.

By the time I caught up and washed the dishes in the bar sink, Paul had arrived. I didn't want to leave the two waitresses without a barista or impose on Sue again, so I suggested to eBeth that we have our meeting at the bar.

"Give me the usual," Paul said, placing a valise I'd never seen before on the bar and taking his seat. "eBeth tells me you've joined the business."

"As a consultant," the girl said hastily. "Unpaid."

I poured my team's technical expert a short glass of the single malt I imported specially from Earth for him and gave eBeth an orange juice. "So what's the new business, Paul?"

"Licensing. Without patent protection, there's no point in building a giant factory, and Stacey told me that she doesn't want to see this village turned into a manufacturing city like some of the places she takes the locals on her Earth tours."

"I don't understand. Without patent protection, why would anybody pay for a license?"

"I'm not going to license the inventions, Mark, I'm going to license operators. We've been training boiler firemen informally for the last year and Peter suggested making a business of it. That means prep books, test sheets, and certificates."

"Have you run this past the guild?" I asked.

"What guild? The closest thing to a supervisory body on this planet is the board of the Engineer's Journal, and the only one of their magazines that even touches on steam is the edition for mill engineers."

"And they're focused almost entirely on water power," I confirmed, having subscribed to the magazine myself. "So you're going to set up an independent certification school?"

"Why not? Half of the home owners around here have been adding rooms to their houses to board people coming for the tourist school, and there are two new rooming houses going up in the village, if you haven't noticed. I thought I was going to have to build a dormitory, but I'd rather spread the wealth and not get stuck playing company town. It's like you said a couple of months ago. Just because these people are open to change doesn't mean we should shove it down their throats. We should do our best to make sure that whatever we leave behind when we move on is self-sustainable."

"Test prep books are perfect for us," eBeth said happily. "I don't know if you'll actually want to print test sheets because the setup is expensive and you won't want to use the same ones over and over again."

"Why not?" Paul and I asked at the same time.

"Because people cheat," eBeth told us. "It's not just an Earth thing, either. Think about it. If you had a friend taking a test that you had already passed, and you knew that the questions hadn't change, wouldn't you share?"

"I'd teach my friend enough to pass the test without cheating," Paul said, and I nodded my agreement.

"Humans don't all have your capacity for learning," the girl said seriously. "I've noticed that about you guys. You never look at a problem and ask for help. You just dig in and start working."

"I ask for your help with Sue all the time," I reminded her.

"That's different. All males are clueless about what females want."

"It's just our encounter suits that—" I began, but eBeth hadn't finished yet.

"For you, acquiring knowledge is about clearing enough storage space if you run out," she continued. "It took me six months just to learn enough New Aramaic to

167

get by, and after two years, I'm still not fluent. How long did it take you?"

"You know languages are a hobby with me," I said, feeling oddly embarrassed.

"And you?" eBeth demanded of Paul.

"I just downloaded the vocabulary and syntax from him," my oldest friend said, throwing me under the bus. "How about certificates? Are you printing in color yet?"

The curveball threw eBeth for a loop. "We've only printed black so far."

"A letterpress isn't a laser printer or an inkjet, eBeth," I said, jumping on the opportunity to change the subject. "It will print whatever color ink you use."

"I guess we've only bought black so far."

"Certificates and diplomas usually use multiple colors," Paul informed her. "With your press, that means running the same sheets again with new ink after swapping in the new type or woodcut."

"That's not a problem," she said. "Bob's doing that now to print advertising on the back of the necktie instructions. He'll just have to put the paper in with the same side up."

"Arrrrgh," a boy's voice cried in anguish, and all conversation in the café came to a sudden stop. The only remaining sounds were the regular mechanical whirrs and clunks from the letterpress.

"It's alright," Naomi called out immediately. "He didn't cut himself. It's just the tail."

"Just the tail?" Monos cried indignantly. "I've been carving this pony all afternoon, and now his tail isn't attached to his butt."

"Bring it over here," I told him as a dozen conversations picked up again. "And bring the tools you're using as well."

"I can't thank you enough for the pony, Mr. Ai," Naomi said as soon as the two of them reached the bar. "I'm going to keep saving so I can pay you back if you change your mind. You really didn't have to buy me a present just because you gave Monos those tools."

eBeth glared at me over the girl's shoulder, so I suppressed the urge to pretend I was accepting her offer of reimbursement.

"It's my pleasure, Naomi. Let me see that block, Monos."

"Here, and what she said."

I examined the woodcutting and found myself as impressed by the boy's artistic ability as by his carving skill. "This isn't a problem, Monos. We just have to cut out a small wedge where you slipped, drive in a plug, and you'll be able to shave that down to match." I inspected the tools and paused on the gouge that matched the width of the unintended amputation of the pony's tail. "Is this your favorite gouge?" I asked, testing the sharpness on my thumb.

"He uses it for everything," Naomi interjected.

"We need to find you a contoured sharpening stone for honing the gouge before you use it, and I'll make up a leather cylinder for stropping as well," I told the boy. "The sharper you keep your tools, the less likely they'll catch the grain or a flaw in the wood and make a sudden turn on you."

"What's the difference between sharpening, honing and stropping?"

"Honing is just sharpening with a fine stone," Paul explained.

"Don't listen to him, he's a machinist," I said. "Honing maintains the cutting edge while sharpening removes steel to create a new edge. Stropping is more like polishing, and if you're using the same tool for hours, you should stop from time to time and polish the edge."

"You're getting to be a real mentor," eBeth complimented me.

I actually froze for a moment, my mouth agape.

"A mentor carries extra significance for AI," Paul explained to her. "It can imply parentage."

"Do you mean that Mark's mentor is actually his father?" the girl demanded.

"What did I miss?" Sue asked, slipping past the waitress station and setting a tray of cookies on the bar for the children. "That's a lovely pony, Monos. I look forward to seeing it printed."

"Mr. Ai is going to help me fix the tail," the boy told her. "eBeth says that he's my mentor."

"And how's he doing so far?" Sue asked without batting an eye.

"He's pretty good," Monos admitted. "He bought me all these tools and gave Naomi a pony. We're going to print invitations for her birthday party with a pony on them."

"Why don't you finish putting the barn in the background and then we'll do the repair," I suggested. The boy nodded his agreement, and after gathering up his tools and the large woodblock with the girl's help, the two of them headed back to their table next to the letterpress.

"Nobody answered my question," eBeth said, pointing a finger at me. "The first time I met your mentor on Earth, he introduced himself as your father, or the closest thing to it."

"And I told you he was my mentor. The two aren't mutually exclusive, and the concept of fatherhood doesn't mean the same thing with artificial intelligence as it does for biological reproduction."

"So do you share programming or something?"

"It's not that simple, eBeth, and programming, by its very definition, can never lead to sentience. Some robots have programming so sophisticated that they can outperform people at any task you set them, but they would never choose to create something new of their own accord."

"Like some of the worlds on the portal system set up by the Originals where the robot makers have died off and the robots couldn't evolve."

"Exactly. Programmed behavior is just that. The League uses the term 'artificial intelligence' to denote sentient entities that weren't born of biological reproduction. Back on Earth, your people use artificial intelligence to describe computer programs that do anything which was once thought impossible, like understanding human speech, playing chess, or driving a car."

"But did your mentor help create you?" eBeth persisted.

"You can ask the next time you see him," I told her.

"Hi, Mark," an attractive middle-aged woman said, taking the stool next to the waitress station. "My niece says she's making money hand-over-foot."

I flashed a triumphant look at Sue before replying to Delilah's aunt.

"Can I get you anything, Lilith, or are you here to see Bob?"

"Both," she said. "I'll have an espresso, and then I'm taking him out to dinner as soon as this one lets him off work."

"He can leave whenever you want," eBeth told her generously. "We use time sheets."

Fifteen

Despite all of my previous promises to myself, at the last minute, standing in front of the second floor closet, I found myself asking Sue, "Are you sure you have to go?"

"It's only for the rest of the summer, Mark. I'll be back in less than two months."

"How am I going to run the travel agency and the café without you?"

"Helen is here and she's a better baker than I am. She has my latest memories from our portal business, and Stacey can help out when she's not leading a tour group on Earth."

"Stop whining, Mark," eBeth said. "Don't you want Sue to leave with a positive impression?"

"I thought it over and I don't want her to leave at all," I whined.

"Keep him out of trouble, eBeth, and don't let him spend all of his savings on being mayor," Sue said. Then she gave me a quick kiss on the lips and vanished through the portal with her single rollaway. My second-in-command had always been a good packer.

"That was pathetic," eBeth said, closing the closet door and shooing me away towards the stairs. "Even Spot was embarrassed."

I looked over at the Archmage, who had come upstairs to see Sue off, and he nodded his agreement. My shoulders slumped.

"It's just that she's never left me before."

"No, you always leave her," eBeth said. "Like every month when you go on one of your scouting missions and she doesn't know if you'll come back in one piece."

"It's not the same," I protested. "That's my job."

Spot snorted and headed back downstairs, but eBeth stood waiting for me.

"What?" I asked.

"Sue told me to keep you out of trouble and I've decided that you're acting too flaky to leave by yourself. You'll probably go in the bedroom and fondle her clothes or something weird like that."

"You wait until Peter takes off somewhere for two months and leaves you behind," I grumbled, allowing myself to be herded down the stairs. "We'll see how you like it."

"He'll never do that because I'll kill him first. Come on. Let's check the suggestion box."

"Do we have to?" I was beginning to see how whining got to be a habit with some people. It seemed to create a negative feedback loop that led to an odd feeling of satisfaction. I made a note to investigate later.

"It will take your mind off of Sue," eBeth told me firmly. When we reached the foot of the stairs, I stuck my arm out the front door and retrieved the "Suggestions for the mayor" box from its position of honor next to the boot scraper that helped reduce the mud tracked in during bad weather. Then I joined eBeth in the café, where she had taken over the table nearest to the printing press to supervise her business empire.

"Morning, Bob," I greeted the ex-policeman, who was pumping away on the treadle. "Still printing ads on the backs of our tie instructions?"

"Finished that job yesterday. I've moved on to Paul's first test-prep book for boiler firemen. It's interesting stuff, but I'd hate to be standing next to one if I did the math wrong and it blew up."

"Bob can help with the suggestions," eBeth said. "He's an expert in municipal government."

"I put in my time," he allowed modestly. "What's the problem?"

"Everybody has their own pet project that they want the town to finish yesterday," I explained, hoping it didn't sound like I was whining.

"Have you found out what the budget is yet?"

"The town of Covered Bridge doesn't have one. We're too new."

"Can you estimate from the revenue stream?"

"Zero," I replied.

"Ouch," Bob said. "I think you're going to be running a deficit your first year. Can you borrow?"

"I wish. I read the rules and the mayor has no authority to sign promissory notes committing the town."

"Hey, guys," Helen said, pulling out a chair and taking a seat with us. "Did Sue assign you to keep an eye on him, eBeth? While the cat's away, the mice will play."

"This mouse would be curled up in his nest crying in his ale if I let him have his way," eBeth told her.

"There's the first useful piece of advice I've heard today," I said, getting up and heading for the bar. "I'll drown my sorrows."

"It's morning, Mark," Bob called after me. "You know what they say about people who drink in the morning."

"I won't turn on Kim's inebriation algorithm," I lied, and drew myself a tankard from the keg. "Sue specifically told me not to spend all of my money taking care of town business. Any ideas how we can raise funds?"

"We could have a bake sale," Helen suggested brightly.

"To pay for enough cobblestones to pave the road?"

"How about our eponymous covered bridge?" eBeth asked, deploying a word I doubt she had ever used out loud, unless it was in one of her English classes. "Who paid to redo the roof last year?"

"The provincial government. Even though it's a dirt road through town, it's part of the provincial system." I retook my seat before I realized I hadn't asked if anybody else wanted anything. I must have been taking Sue's leaving even harder than I realized. "Does anybody else—"

"We just had breakfast. How come I can't get the lid of the suggestion box open?"

"I had to put in a few screws," I told her, reaching in my pocket and pulling out a Torx bit, the only one on the planet. "The first week I thought it was a little odd that I was getting exactly one suggestion a day, but then Justin showed me the security footage from their camera across the street. Every time somebody came to put in a suggestion, they cleaned out the box first."

"That's pretty low," Bob said, as I removed the two screws that secured the lid from being opened. "Still, at least the townspeople are engaged."

"Wow! There must be a hundred pieces of paper crammed in here," eBeth exclaimed. "These are all from one day?"

"I may have let it go for a week or so because I was trying to spend as much time as possible with Sue," I admitted.

"Maybe this won't be so bad," she said after unfolding a few scraps of paper. "The first two I picked were repeats.

175

Why don't we make a separate pile for each request, and then you can analyze the handwriting and find out how many of the suggestions in every pile are from the same person?"

"This one is for an aqueduct," Helen announced, smoothing a note on the table.

"Just toss it," I told her. "The capital is the only city in the province with an aqueduct. It's not just that we'll never be able to afford one, we don't need one either."

"Filling the rooftop tank is easy for you, Mark, but I'm sure that some of the older folks in town would make running water their top priority," Bob pointed out, while pumping away on the treadle with his right foot. I have to admit that it was a pleasure to watch him work the press, though sometimes he seemed to be flirting with getting his fingers crushed while replacing a freshly printed sheet with new stock. "Maybe Paul could rig a steam engine to power a town well rather than everybody having to pump their own."

"I think a water tower would make more sense," I mused, "but even then you're talking about a lot of money to run pipes to all of the houses, and the only people who get the benefit are the ones with homes in the center of town. Most of the population live on the surrounding farms, and there's never going to be enough money to run water pipes all the way out to their places."

"This one is requesting a water tower," eBeth said, placing the note on the table between herself and Helen. "Add the aqueduct enthusiast and this pile can be all things water."

"And this will be the streetlight pile," Helen declared, laying down a new request. "The person specified that they want gas lamps like the city, but that's probably not in the budget."

"Nothing is in the budget," I reiterated, mainly as a caution to myself. "The only thing that would make sense at this point is to put out oil lanterns like Justin's and get volunteers to go around every evening to light them and do the maintenance."

"I could do that," Helen offered immediately. "While I'm in town, anyway."

"And who pays for the lanterns and the oil?" Bob asked.

"A couple dozen would take care of our commercial district," I said, referring to the restaurants and shops, of which my café was an anchor business. "Maybe if I bought the lanterns the owners of each building would agree to pay for oil and take turns lighting them."

"And there's no point burning oil all night like Kim and Justin do," eBeth said. "I'd suggest putting out all the lanterns after the restaurants and the café close because nobody but the Originals come through here at night."

"Here's a good suggestion," Helen said. "Reprogram the Ferrymen's Body to project multi-player games in the temple after hours."

"Let me see that," I demanded. I expected that it would be written in English and match either eBeth's or Peter's handwriting, but the request was neatly printed in Modern Aramaic.

"I've got another one," eBeth said, handing me a similar note.

"Which one of these did you write," I asked Helen.

"Neither. You haven't found any of mine yet, and I put one in every day I've been here."

Something about the neatness of the printing rang a bell, and I realized the author was Art, just as the Original entered the café with Monos and Naomi.

"Did somebody pay you to stuff the suggestion box?" I inquired.

"I'm just glad to know that you're finally reading them," Art responded through his pendant. "eBeth told me that she met Peter through playing games back on Earth, and it always struck me as silly that the Ferrymen's temples go largely unused at night."

"I want to play Earth games," Monos said. "eBeth told us about all the monsters and they sounded just like ours."

"He means from the role-playing games we play with dice and cards," Naomi interpreted for me.

"Well, it wouldn't cost anything," I ventured, "and you are constituents, even if you aren't old enough to vote."

"We are old enough to vote," Naomi told me. "Twelve is the cut-off. It's just that those meetings are so boring that nobody our age ever goes."

"I can't fault you there. Let's work through the rest of these suggestions and then I'll head over to the Ferrymen's temple and have a look at the encryption. Will you be available to help if there's a magical lock, Art?"

"I can try, but the Archmage would be the better choice."

"He left to escape Mark's pity fest," eBeth told the Original, and without pausing to give me a chance to defend myself, added, "Free espressos for everybody."

"You don't like espresso and it's not good for children," I said.

"I didn't mean us, I was reading a suggestion."

"This note is asking for free bus rides for everybody," Helen said.

"Why aren't there any offers to help make the town a better place?" I asked. "If one of you were elected mayor, that's what I would put in the box."

"Negotiate a sponsorship deal with the Originals," eBeth read.

"That's a great idea. Would you be willing, Art?"

"I better be, since that's one of the notes I put in."

"That makes it an even better idea. But what would you want in return?"

"We've already got it," the Original said. "Your bringing us the Archmage and arranging with Pffift to import magical supplies is more than enough reason for us to support you. And your head librarian offered to let me use Library's communications infrastructure to broadcast a message to my kind updating them on the success of our experiment."

"So you're willing to pay for paving stones or a water tower?"

"It's well within our means to pay for both, Mark. We'll just be returning the money that the Ferrymen tithed from the inhabitants to pay rent for being on Reservation because we were here first."

"So what's the difference between a sponsorship and a gift?" eBeth asked.

"Sponsorships come with strings attached," Art explained to her. "First, the projects we finance get plaques showing that we paid for them."

"You can carve it into every cobblestone for all I care," I told him happily. "Paint it on the water tower and on the lanterns."

"I thought you were going to buy the lanterns," eBeth objected.

"That was before I landed the town a sponsorship deal. What other suggestions are there?"

"They mainly repeat," Helen said. "Water, road, streetlights, gaming. Oh, and both of your waitresses want me to open a pole-dancing school in town."

"How do you know it's them?"

"They signed their suggestions. Do you want me to get you a refill?"

I finally noticed that I'd been trying to drink from an empty tankard, so I got up and went to pour myself another. I had to admit that I was feeling much better already. "Anything for you, Art?"

"Not until we get a look at the encryption on the Ferryman's Body," he said. "Alcohol reduces the effectiveness of my magic."

"Finished," eBeth announced while my back was turned. "There's no need to count the notes in the piles. Running water, paving the road, and streetlights were the three big winners."

"Rome wasn't built in a day," Bob said. "I don't claim to be a city planner, but I'd bury a water main first so you don't have to dig up all the cobblestones after laying them. If you hang the lanterns on brackets attached to the existing structures, they'll be out of the way."

"I'll have to go around and talk to everybody on Main Street to make sure they're all on board," I said, setting my tankard in the sink rather than refilling it. "Some people might prefer the road as it is."

"You're the mayor," eBeth told me. "You don't go door-to-door. Write something up and I'll print it. The kids can distribute the flyers, and then you can hold a public meeting in the café."

"On a Tuesday night," I added.

"So let's get going," eBeth said, stuffing all of the suggestions in the recycling bin. "I want to kill some monsters."

"Aren't there any nice games you could play? I thought you liked the one with the farm and—"

"When I was thirteen I liked it. Naomi and Monos live on farms. For them it would be like doing chores."

"I want to be a mage, like Art or Spot," Monos declared, choosing as unlikely a pair of role models as a human boy could find.

"You can't be a mage," Naomi told him. "You can be a wizard."

"What's the difference?"

"Mages have innate power, wizards work magic with enchanted objects and spells," she explained.

"And demons," eBeth added.

"I don't mind broadening your entertainment horizons but I hope you can remember that none of it is real," I told the kids.

"Art's real," Monos said. "He does magic all the time."

"Obviously, I didn't mean Art or Spot," I backtracked. "I'm talking about demons and necromancers, the made-up characters in role-playing games."

"What's a necromancer?" Naomi asked.

"I'll tell you on the way," eBeth said, getting up and heading for the door. "See you later, Bob. Should I bring the new game controllers I bought in Boston, Mark?"

"You brought them here?"

"I wasn't going to leave them on Earth, was I?"

"You may as well," I said after a moment's reflection. "I suppose you have some game DVDs?"

"I'll pick something that doesn't require an Internet connection, but how are you going to read a DVD?"

181

"Did you bring your laptop?"

"The one you upgraded with a Bereftian computing core that's got more processing power than a cloud data center? You told me to leave it in your office on Earth because it's illegal to import it to a non-League world."

"If you're going to play games without one of my team present, you'll need something to run the operating system, and it's torture for us to emulate Windows," I told her. "I can read a DVD by spinning it and squinting, but it's not my idea of a good time.

"Lucky for us I ignored you," eBeth said. "You guys go ahead and I'll catch up with you at the temple."

"I'll help you carry," Helen offered.

"Just let me get my sketchbook," Monos said. It took him a while to find it under the pile of drawings and half-finished woodblocks he was preparing for Paul. By the time all of the test-prep materials were printed, I was guessing that the boy would be qualified as a boiler fireman himself from having carved all of the illustrations.

"Did you really not know that eBeth brought back a computer from Earth?" Art asked me as we strolled towards the Ferrymen's temple. "My own radio frequency detection is limited in this body, but the noise that processor makes is pretty difficult to miss."

"Sue told me to pretend I didn't know," I explained. "Now that you mention it, I hope nothing important comes up with eBeth while Sue is away because I always counted on her to tell me what to do about the girl."

"I thought Helen was older than either of you. Couldn't she help?"

I glanced around to make sure eBeth and my team member hadn't caught up with us yet before replying. "Helen is usually part of the problem."

Sixteen

"What's with the heavy coat in the middle of the summer?" I asked the Hanker.

"Art told me to bring it since we're trekking up into the hills."

"Looks like overkill to me."

"I wish I was going with you but somebody has to mind the café," Helen said. She handed Pffift the digital camera our travel agency used in producing phony documents for tourists. "eBeth wants somebody to take pictures."

"We'll probably be back in time for the evening rush," I told her. "The location Art described is only about an hour from here, and the ride back is downhill."

"Why not ask Peter to give us a lift part way in the bus?" the Hanker suggested.

"Going by your gut, you can use the exercise, Pffift. I know your brain hasn't gotten that much bigger."

We mounted our bicycles, and then I led the way out of town and into the hills, keeping the pace moderate for my companion. Following Art's detailed instructions, we soon ended up on a path I'd never taken before and rode for almost three-quarters of an hour through the woods. We were climbing most of the way, leaving Pffift with little excess wind for conversation, though he did his best to try. Finally we arrived at a large rock that had been split in two.

"Art said to leave our bikes here and hike the rest of the way," I told the Hanker, dismounting and leaning my bicycle against the rock.

"Do you have a chain?"

"What for? You're not worried that somebody is going to come all the way up here and steal your bike, are you? We're pretty far off the beaten path."

"We're one step off a beaten path," Pffift observed. "Let's at least hide them. You have to meet life halfway."

I didn't really think it was necessary, but I followed his lead and carried my bicycle around to the other side of the landmark. Strangely enough, there was a chain anchored into the rock with a combination lock on the end. Apparently somebody else had seen the need to secure a bicycle against theft.

"What are you doing?" I asked the Hanker. He held the lock to his ear and began to fiddle with the dial.

"Here." Pffift thrust the end of the chain with the lock at me. "I almost had it before you started talking. Let's see what that super hearing of yours can do."

Picking the combination lock took me exactly one try, which should have made Pffift wonder how secure it really was. I didn't want to waste time arguing, so I let him lock our bikes together while I did a quick radar scan of the slope to find the cavern entrance Art had described.

"It's this way," I told the Hanker, starting off up a narrow trail.

"Are these stones supposed to be stairs?" he complained. "They're more in the way than helpful."

"It's just until we get to the cave."

"I don't do caves," Pffift said, poking me in the shoulder from behind. "There are always things living in them that don't appreciate unwelcome houseguests."

"I'll warn you if there are any threats inside. Since when are you afraid of anything?"

"I'm not afraid, I'm enlightened. Have you ever played 'Caverns of Chaos and Despair?'"

"Let me guess. You were out at the Ferrymen temple last night with eBeth and Peter."

"Helen was there too—we played teams. I'm just saying that only a fool goes into a cavern unprepared. I don't even have any healing potions with me."

"Piggyback," I offered.

"What did you call me?"

"I'll carry you. According to Art, the path we take through the cave will bring us out on the other side in ten minutes, and it will save almost an hour of climbing over the ridge."

"If I knew we were going on an adventure I would have brought a rope."

"You can't prepare for everything, Pffift," I said, coming to a halt in front of the cavern's dark entrance. "Climb on my back and try not to squirm around."

"My brain isn't going to like this," the Hanker grumbled as he climbed onto the back of my encounter suit. He locked his arms around my neck so tightly that I would have suffocated if I actually needed to breathe. I reached down with my hands and supported each of his legs behind the knee. "And don't bang my head on anything in the dark," he added.

"It's not dark for me," I assured him. "In addition to infrared, I've activated my radar and sonar. I have a clearer vision of what's going on inside this cave than I do in broad daylight."

"That sounds like what the man said before he stepped into the sewer that was missing the manhole cover," Pffift retorted. Seven minutes later he asked, "Are we there yet?"

"Three more minutes by my reckoning, unless you want me to jog."

The Hanker didn't deign to reply, but when we emerged from the cavern a few minutes later he looked around and whistled his approval. "That was worth the ride."

We found ourselves in a small valley with steep slopes rising on every side. The land had been cleared and planted with grass except for a ring of trees that had somehow been woven together as they grew, creating a giant circular wall.

"The Originals must have been preparing this place for some time," I said. "Art described it as their magic academy."

"Then what are we waiting for?" Pffift strode through the gap between two tree trunks, and I almost ran into his back following because he stopped dead. The interior space was packed with more Originals than I had ever seen at one place at one time, thousands of them. Fortunately, Art was wearing his telepathy-to-speech pendant, which made it possible to locate him electronically.

"What do you think they're all doing?" my companion asked, displaying a rare sign of nerves. "Why don't any of them react to us?"

"You know they aren't big talkers. My guess is that Spot is giving a lecture via telepathy and they're all listening."

"You wouldn't see me welcoming the Archmage into my head even if I could," Pffift said, but I noticed that he spoke in a whisper that I barely picked up myself.

Art somehow figured out that we had arrived, or maybe Spot tipped him off, and he began working his way out through the crowd on a course to intercept us. At the same time, all of the Originals began clearing their throats as if preparing for a big performance.

"Are they going to sing?" Pffift asked in disbelief. "I've heard Art try, and when he's really on his game he sounds like a large animal in pain."

"Be ready to stick something in your ears," I warned him, before turning to greet the approaching Original. "Thanks for inviting us, Art. Are you about to have a group sing?"

"Our sensei has been teaching us weather magic. We're going to make it snow."

"Why? Even if you can make it happen, the snow will never stick in this weather."

"You underestimate the Archmage," Art informed me gravely. "His magic isn't limited to penetrating encrypted information systems. He says that statistics quantify the improbable, but magic explains the impossible."

The soft howling of the Originals began to pick up volume, and together with Pffift I backed away towards the barrier of trees. Art followed, but I could tell he was torn between playing the good host and joining in the cacophony.

"Don't you guys know any quiet magic?" the Hanker asked.

"Certainly, but singing is required for the most powerful incantations. It was one of our design considerations in the guided evolution of these bodies."

"But you sound awful."

"We're just warming up," Art said. "Besides, it's about staying in tune and hitting the right harmonics. You can't judge us according to your own musical preferences."

"How many different Originals are represented in this powwow?" I asked.

"Four of us are here with practically all of our clones, and it's a relief to have most of my mind within easy speaking distance for a change. Another eleven of us are here in smaller numbers. The Archmage only gave us a week's notice to prepare, and the transportation systems on this world don't facilitate flash magical convocations."

"You should learn teleportation," Pffift said straight-faced.

"You're making fun of us, but to the extent that anybody understands the crystal transports, that's probably a fair description of how they operate. Our best guess is that the retrieval webs represent a stored form of teleportation magic tied to a particular matrix of the space-time continuum."

"You mean that when the mages sing to the crystal to extract the web, they're essentially saving up teleportation energy for future use?" I asked. "But I'm not aware of any magical species achieving teleportation."

"Powerful mages can displace small objects over modest distances," Art said. "A weak practitioner like myself can transfer something I'm touching, like draining ale from your keg, but that's of limited utility. By amassing teleportation magic over a long period of time, the way the mages on Eniniac do by singing to a crystal in relays for years, transporting individuals becomes possible."

"But why make it snow in the middle of the summer?" Pffift asked, buttoning up his heavy coat because the temperature was already beginning to drop. "Is it a basic exercise for thermodynamic control?"

"The Archmage informed us that this is a necessary step on the road to enlightenment."

"He tells everybody the same thing about rubbing his belly," I pointed out.

"There," Art said, pointing at the sky. Grey clouds were materializing out of thin air and blocking the sun, further lowering the temperature at ground level. "It should only take a few minutes now. You may want to place your hands over your ears, Pffift."

I turned the gain on my hearing down to zero, rendering myself effectively deaf. Then it struck me that the head librarian would no doubt be willing to barter plenty of information for a recording of the Originals singing a magical chorus under the direction of the Archmage of Eniniac, and I reluctantly increased the gain.

If the song had words, I was unable to pick them out. My instrumentation suite began reporting possible fault codes as the weather developed more rapidly than natural phenomena would allow. Snow began to fall heavily, and the acoustics in the enclosed valley underwent a rapid change, with the noise that the Originals were making almost starting to sound like music. The singing went on until the snow was higher than my knees, and then the sound and snowfall stopped as abruptly as if somebody had flipped a switch.

"Is it over?" Pffift asked, removing a hand from one of his ears.

"Our assignment has been completed successfully," Art informed us proudly. "The Archmage is on his way."

"Spot's coming to see us?" It finally occurred to me to pull out my dosimeter badge to see if I'd taken a magical overdose from the singing, but apparently the weather magic of the Originals wasn't of the same type as the Archmage's natural aura. Something cold and soft hit me in the back, and I turned just in time to be met by a flurry of snowballs thrown by Art's clones.

"That was uncalled for," Pffift said, helping to brush the snow off the front of my thin summer shirt. He turned to the Originals and demanded, "Who threw those?"

As I expected, the clones all pointed at each other. Some things never change. Then the wall of bodies parted like the Red Sea, and Spot came trotting through, looking inordinately pleased with himself. Even I had to admit that the cask he was wearing around his neck didn't look so out of place now that the ground was covered with snow, though that was already trampled down in the area where the Originals had been milling about and singing.

"The Archmage has a special request for you," Art announced through his speaking pendant. "If we could step outside and speak in private."

"We're already outside," I grumbled, but I followed Art and Spot through a gap between two of the woven tree trunks. The pupils of my artificial eyes shrank to pinpoints as the now-brilliant sun shone off the snow-covered slopes, creating a blinding wall of light.

"I knew I should have brought snow goggles," Pffift berated himself. "It was my first instinct when Art recommended the winter coat, and you should always go with your first instincts."

"eBeth tells me to do the opposite," I said, though even I was having trouble focusing on much. "What do you want, Spot?"

"The Archmage would like you to run up the slope a bit and then fall down," Art told me in his role as a telepathic

190

translator. "He'll come from the opposite direction to meet you."

"Excuse me?"

"And we should do this quickly because everybody else wants to come out and enjoy the snow as well. You brought the camera, Pffift?"

"Helen gave it to me," the Hanker said, pulling the camera out of his pocket.

A creeping suspicion rose through my processors, and I asked, "Is the whole point of this exercise, weather magic and all, to get a picture of Spot coming with his cask to rescue me?"

"He knew you'd understand," Art said. "I believe he's already talked with the local Ferrymen's agent to commission a number of rugs on the general theme, so we'd like to get a variety of poses."

I glared at the dog, but I didn't want to go down as the worst bad sport in Reservation's history, and after thousands of Originals had poured their magical and musical talents into creating the snowy set for the photo shoot, I was trapped. Unless, that is, Pffift was the one being rescued.

"It's going to be tricky getting the exposure right against a pure white background," I told the Hanker disingenuously. "You better override the automatic settings and shoot on manual. Think you can do that?"

"Good point," Pffift said, handing over the camera. Then he stripped off his coat and passed that to me as well. "Put this on or the pictures will look like somebody staged them in the middle of the summer. And give the camera back. You must have forgotten that I was a tourist on Earth. I've probably taken more snow photographs than you have."

Given that my experience with the camera was limited to shooting false passport pictures in front of my café, it was possible that he wasn't lying. I shrugged into the coat, did the buttons, and crouched down to look the Archmage in the eye. "You owe me, Spot. I didn't ask for anything after finding out that you'd been rooting around in my mind for over three years and blocking my memories, but playing the part of a man lost in the Alps is beyond reasonable."

"He says you better get going before the snow melts," Art told me as Spot bounded off to the right, taking high leaps more like a deer than a dog to minimize the amount of time his undercarriage was pressed in the snow.

I did a quick estimate of the maximum field of view for the camera lens in case Pffift took a shot at the minimum zoom, and then set off on the proper vector. When I saw the Archmage changing his angle to intercept me, I gave a dramatic cry and collapsed in the snow. A minute later, I felt a warm tongue licking my face and sat bolt upright.

"Was that really necessary?" I demanded.

Spot panted happily with exertion, his tail whacking out a half of a snow-angel behind him, and he placed his front paws on my thighs so he could stand up higher to give the photographer a better profile.

"That's great," Art called to me. "Reach for the cask like you're going to unbuckle it from around his neck. No, you don't have to keep your face towards the camera, Mark. Pay attention to what you're doing."

We took a brief break while Art and Pffift reviewed the pictures that the Hanker had taken so far, and then the Original started up with his directions again.

"We want to get one where you're snow-blind and he's leading you to safety. Do you have something to tie over your eyes?"

"No," I called back.

"There's a scarf in one of the pockets," Pffift shouted helpfully.

I sighed and wrapped the scarf around my eyes, and then took hold of the cask's strap at the back of Spot's neck. "Try not to lead us both into a chasm," I told him.

For whatever the reason, the Archmage chose to guide me away from the camera, rather than towards it, maybe to create the effect of a brave St Bernard guiding a stranded traveler back towards a mountain pass. The snow grew deeper at the foot of the slope and it was becoming an effort for Spot to break the path. I hadn't thought of him as the type to sacrifice himself for art, but I suppose you don't become the leader of a planet of mages without paying dues.

"Perfect," Art shouted across the snow. "You stay there, Mark, and the Archmage is going to come back here for a minute. He wants us to get one of him digging you out of an avalanche."

I whipped off the scarf, noted Spot bounding through the snow back towards the tree-circle magic academy, and then examined the steep slope with snow-penetrating radar. "I'm afraid he's out of luck," I called back. "The snow is stable and it's already starting to melt in the sun. I think we're going to have to call it—"

A deep base howl rose from the throats of thousands of Originals, sending vibrations through my encounter suit down to the very toes. "Or, not," I said to myself as the snow began moving down the slope.

"Maybe you better run back towards us a bit," Art instructed me, his pendant operating at top volume. "We don't want you buried so deep that Spot will be invisible digging you out."

I gritted my teeth and sprinted back towards the trees, my head turned over my shoulder to eyeball the approaching wall of snow. I realized that the Archmage probably wanted the broken snow from the avalanche as a backdrop more than he actually wanted to dig, so I estimated the distance where the snow would end up right around hip-level. Then I lay down on my back and dug in my heels and hands so I wouldn't get tumbled. After the snow rolled over me, I lifted one arm straight up, and was pleased to find I'd calculated correctly. My fingers were in the clear.

Hold that pose, Art transmitted via the radio frequency waves his body was capable of producing organically. *The Archmage will be with you shortly.*

Before a minute was up, I felt Spot nosing around my fingers, and then I heard him digging in a showy doggy manner, flinging the snow between his legs. I figured he'd stop as soon as Pffift had a few shots, but apparently the Archmage was enjoying the unaccustomed exercise, because he continued right on until he was scraping the snow off my chest and only his tail could have been showing above ground. Then he scrambled out of the hole, grabbed the sleeve of my coat in his teeth, and pulled.

A little cooperation would be appreciated, Art sent.

I levered myself up and out of the snow in the direction that Spot was pulling, and wasn't surprised when he eased up just as my head broke the surface, allowing Pffift to bracket exposures. Then the embarrassing photo shoot was over and the Originals poured out into the rapidly melting snow to engage in the biggest snowball fight I'd ever witnessed. Sometimes there's just no understanding superior intellects.

Seventeen

"You've been smuggling in wireless keyboards with built-in game controllers from Earth?" I asked Stacey. "How many?"

"Two hundred so far. They aren't heavy, but the retail packaging takes up a lot of space. And they include a mouse function too, so they're officially three-in-ones."

"And what is eBeth doing with all of these—don't tell me."

"I'm going to show you," she said. "Did you think I was dragging you out to the Ferrymen's temple on a Friday night to watch home movies?"

"I only agreed to come because Bob offered to tend bar in the café. Why do I suspect that Sue asked all of you to keep me out of trouble?"

"Because it's true, but this is also about getting you up to speed on the impact we're having on the locals. After you hacked into the 'My Life' editing station to display the video from eBeth's laptop, it only took Helen a couple of days to get bored with playing two-on-two."

"I know she got addicted to massively multi-player games on Earth, but you need an Internet connection and a data center, not to mention a massive number of players."

"Thanks to the laptop you upgraded for eBeth with a Bereftian core, Helen has it emulating everything. I had to bring in a couple of battery-powered routers—"

"Helen is running a local copy of the Internet in the Ferrymen's temple for the sake of playing MMORPG's?"

"It's some sort of hybrid type of gaming she hacked together that allows everybody to share the same screen. The locals love it, even though they don't get to see the action from the perspective of their own player, but they haven't been spoiled by growing up with first-person shooter games."

"If you call that being spoiled," I said, pulling the door open for Stacey to enter the Ferrymen's temple. Most of the crowd was between the ages of fifteen and forty, though I spotted a few grey-hairs as well. There was some sort of dungeon dive projected on the front wall of the hall, and I could see that all of the avatars were wearing numbered bibs over their armor so the players could easily track their characters.

"It looks like a marathon with monsters and weapons," I couldn't help commenting. "What happens if a player tries moving their character beyond the screen area?"

"They're out of the game unless they can blindly retrace their steps or the frame moves to include them. See how the scope is creeping forward with the flow of the battle?"

"That really is clever. You know, I was never particularly interested in playing games, but..."

"I brought an extra pair of controllers," Stacey said, leading us to a pair of open seats and pulling the units out of her large purse. "I've played this dungeon before and the boss is going to come out of the sarcophagus any time now. See the blank bar to the right of the projection area?" She tapped a few keys on her controller's compact keyboard, and a small but legible registration window opened in the border area.

"I thought it was just a filler bar to match the game resolution to the projector," I said, mimicking her keystrokes. A second window opened, and by the time I worked my way through building a rudimentary character, the triumphant adventurers had finished off the super-powered mummy and were looting everything in sight. Aramaic text bubbles reporting new levels were popping up all over the front wall of the temple, and then the whole projection was taken over by smaller text boxes in which players were busily assigning points and sending each other messages.

"Alright, everybody," Peter called, waving his wireless controller over his head to gain the crowd's attention. "There are too many players here to enjoy a normal quest, so we thought we'd try a little player-vs-player, melee style. Is everybody in?"

The response was overwhelmingly positive.

"It would be too crazy if we played every man for himself, so we're starting with randomly assigning everybody to one of eight teams. You'll know what team you're on by the color of the number bib that appears on your avatar. Members of your team will share a chat channel that will be live in the bar on the right side of the projection. Sorry we couldn't figure out a way to make it private."

I saw eBeth typing something on the laptop keyboard, and the progress bar that zipped across the screen was a testament to the Bereftian computing core. The main area of the projection was taken over by a large grassy field, and characters began popping into view, in order of their numbered bibs. Stacey's maxed-out elf character wore a ninety-two, and the newbie human paladin I'd chosen to play was the ninety-third avatar to appear. More players must have entered after us because the highest number when the additions stopped was ninety-eight.

"The program built the teams so that everybody's chances are the same, even though four teams have an extra player," Peter announced. "It was either that or use three different shades of green that are almost identical."

"Can we have time to huddle with the others on our team and come up with a strategy?" somebody asked.

"We tried that last week, but everybody made alliances and it took all night to finish," eBeth answered. "Let's just have some fun and then we can hit the next dungeon. Ready?"

Somebody elbowed me hard in the chest, and I looked over to see Pffift grasping a controller, his thumbs poised for action. "Going to get you, sucker," he said out of the side of his mouth.

Then Peter dropped his arm, bringing his own controller into action, and all hell broke loose in the projection. I lost three quarters of my health to a blow from a higher level player in my first encounter before another player on my team engaged the enemy. I was still trying to muster up the aggression to actually launch an offensive strike when a coating of ice took my health to zero.

"Freeze," the Hanker said, and I saw a mage character in the projection blowing imaginary smoke off of his fingertips. Then a giant lizard ran him through with a trident. Even before Pffift's health drained away, the lizard pitch-forked the mage avatar completely out of the display area.

"What goes around comes around," I taunted the Hanker, feeling much better about my own rapid death.

"I don't even know what that thing was," Pffift complained. "Since when does this game include reptilian characters? Who would want to play a walking lizard?"

Something about his question struck a chord, and I jumped up from my seat, scanning the mob of players. Sure enough, standing at the fringe of the garden at the back of the hall was a group of Ferrymen. They weren't holding game controllers, but a quick scan of the spectrum informed me that they had patched into the routers via their ever-present visors and were controlling their avatars through practiced eye movements.

Paul, I transmitted an urgent message. *I have five Ferrymen in the temple.*

Not again, my technical specialist replied with a harmonic groan. *Our detection grid has been glitchy all week due to solar flares. I got frustrated with all the false positives and bumped up the signal-to-noise threshold.*

Is there a giant Ferrymen ark hanging over town?

No, and I wouldn't have missed anything that big, even cloaked. Let me refocus on the surface and—got it. It's a Ferrymen picket ship, I didn't realize they were jump-capable. Must be a high ranking official.

I ran an image comparison against my memory and determined we were dealing with the same five Ferrymen who had showed up at the temple a little over a year earlier.

200

It's the same group of lizard-men who brought the Bintrid high-capacity storage unit that Spot decrypted," I transmitted. *"I'll find out what they want as soon as they're finished."*

Finished what?

Participating in a player-vs-player contest. It looks like the bodyguards are all dead, but the chief killed Pffift and has leveled up several times already.

How's your character doing?

I'll talk to you later.

I saw the avatar of the Ferrymen's chief absorb a flurry of arrows fired by an elven archer, but the mage character on his team erected a magical shield in the nick of time, saving his life. Somebody else on the blue team gave the lizard a health potion and pulled out the arrows. Thanks to the lack of preparation time, coordination between the fighters was crude at best, but the head lizard had lucked onto Helen's team. Stacey was one of the last solo players to fall.

"Don't look, but there are five Ferrymen standing in the back," I muttered in her ear.

She turned immediately and glared daggers at the chief lizard. "He's using a cursed trident. How does a newbie get a weapon like that?"

It was a good question, so I checked the game play and discovered that the leader's henchmen had all strategically sacrificed themselves to him in combat, providing enough points to let him upgrade his trident. It amounted to betraying the teams they'd been assigned to, but Peter hadn't announced any rules.

"He cheated," I told her. "I'm going to talk to him as soon as it's over. The red team can't last much longer."

"That's eBeth's mage character, and the ogre is Athena's boyfriend, Benjy. Oops, was Benjy," Stacey corrected herself as the weakened ogre went down under the combined attack of the Ferryman chief and a troll. eBeth must have been more powerful than the blue team's mage because she held out against the three-to-one odds for almost a minute before succumbing. I suspected Helen was going easy on the girl.

"Victory," screeched the Ferryman, and the lizard in the projection shook his trident above his head. The four bodyguards all congratulated their officer with loud hisses, but while I'm not an expert in the Ferrymen language, I thought I caught an undertone of resentment over being utilized as monster fodder to rapidly level their leader.

"Sky Gods," one of the older members in the hall cried in shock, and the room fell silent. Then the projection shifted back to a grid of text boxes, and the players decided that figuring out why their supposed suzerains had returned to the planet could wait until they assigned the points gained in the melee.

The four lower caste Ferrymen turned their visors towards me as I approached, but the chief was apparently too busy assigning his own ill-gotten points to notice. I stopped at a polite distance and waited. Eventually, the officer let out a sound like gargling gravel, the Ferrymen equivalent of frustration, and removed his visor.

"I should have known it would be one of you Library AI," he said in passable Modern Aramaic, albeit with a sibilant flavor. "Are you responsible for making alterations to the 'My Life' editing station?"

"Yes," I replied, seeing no reason to confuse the situation by bringing up Helen's additions to my initial hack. "The changes don't interfere with its primary function."

"Pshaw," the lizard spat. "I don't care about that. Who owns the rights to this game?"

"The one we just played? It's a hash-up of software from Earth put together by one of my team members. I suppose it's all copyrighted on Earth, but Reservation doesn't recognize intellectual property rights."

"Then it's ours," the Ferryman asserted.

"How did you reach that conclusion?"

"The 'My Life' editing stations were all purchased by us, we just loan them to the temples so that the craftsmen can check that their authentication videos are usable. Possession is ninety-nine and ninety-four hundredths percent of the law."

"It's just a few gigabytes of memory," I told him. "I'll make you a copy."

"What other games do you have?" the Ferryman asked, replacing his visor over his eyes.

"It's not really my thing," I explained. "You'll have to talk to Helen and eBeth."

A long pause went by without an answer, and then I realized that the players in the hall had started another dungeon dive, including the five Ferrymen who had gone rigid. I sighed and returned to my seat to tell Stacey that I'd had enough for the evening and to ask her to bring the Ferrymen by my café when everybody ran out of energy. To my surprise, she was playing her controller on her lap and mine on my seat.

"Hurry up and take it," she said. "I borrowed a mage character from Helen for you—she plays so much that she has spares."

I seized the controller and quickly located my character on the projection by casting a fireball in the air, a stunt which unfortunately compromised our raid party's stealthy approach. As the messages castigating my character's action piled up in the queue on the right side of the projection, skeleton warriors poured out of every nook and cranny of the cavern, and the red pixels began to flow.

I'd never actually played a mage before, but I quickly found that I had a talent for healing. I stuck to getting our wounded warriors back onto their feet, and even found myself reattaching the tail to a reptilian swordsman. Out of the corner of my eye I saw a message with my bib number pop into the top of the message queue, reading, "It would have grown back anyway, but thanks."

The hordes of animated skeletons proved to be less of a threat than I would have expected, and I was beginning to wonder if all dungeons were this easy, when a cry went up that the dungeon boss was materializing. Then I heard eBeth clearly above the general noise, saying, "Oh, no. Not the lich again."

Two things happened almost simultaneously. First, all of the skeletons our band of adventurers had hacked or blown apart somehow reassembled themselves and rose to their feet, but their stats were now much higher. Second, a mage who I recognized as Pffift's character threw a giant icicle at the lich that I was sure would crush the skeleton boss and end the battle. Instead, the lich gestured almost imperceptibly with its staff and the icicle blew back at our forces in a million fragments. Half of our players went down with critical hits.

"Oops," Pffift muttered, as all of the prematurely slaughtered players turned around to glare at him. "Mark, you have to team up with me to kill this lich. It takes mages to deal with dark magic."

"I'm too busy healing icicle wounds," I told him, though the truth was, relatively few players whose armor proved insufficiently leveled to withstand the attack had survived. "Besides, I don't know what I'm doing."

"Cast 'monkey-see, monkey-do' on yourself and then I'll be able to control your character," the Hanker said.

"I'm not casting anything on myself, and why is the lich getting bigger?"

"Now we're in for it," Stacey muttered.

It took me a moment to realize that pieces of the newly revived skeletons we'd been dispatching were now skittering across the floor to the dungeon boss, who was actually growing stronger as we killed its minions.

"How do you beat something like this?" I asked.

The head of the lich's staff began to glow a sickly green, and I heard Peter shouting to the remaining players, "Run away. Run away." Then the whole projection suddenly seemed to melt as if somebody had tossed a huge bucket of slime on the wall, and I heard Peter groan, "We wiped."

"Mark," eBeth called to me, as everybody began a general discussion of what they wanted to play next. "I'll meet you at the back."

I only had to take a few steps towards the exit, but the girl had to make her way through the crowd of gamers to reach me.

"I'm impressed, eBeth," I told her. "I didn't think that so many of the people in town would be interested in video gaming."

"It's just a beta test. Helen wants to roll it out to all of the Ferrymen temples, but that would require importing a lot of alien computer hardware, not to mention figuring out a way to charge batteries without violating the Sky God rules."

"Did you notice that the Ferrymen were here?"

"They're kind of hard to miss, Mark. I was a little worried when they came in, but as soon as I saw the lizard characters signing up for our PVP scrum, I knew they were gamers. I came back here because I want you to introduce me."

"Is this eBethssss?" the Ferrymen's chief hissed at our approach, again removing his visor in a surprising show of politeness.

"Hello, uh, Sky God," eBeth replied in her imperfect Aramaic. "Welcome to open gaming night."

"I understand you have more games."

"Lots, and I know where to get even more. I can't believe how well you did your first time playing."

"We have our own interactive games, but they mainly revolve around farming or galactic trade. Your Earth must be home to many monsters."

"Yes, in a manner of speaking. We'd like to, uh, share those monsters with more people on Reservation."

"Using our editing stations," the Ferryman prompted.

"It seems like the best solution. The people here aren't ready for personal computers in every home, and your rules prohibit electrical generation. We were wondering if you would mind if we imported photovoltaic panels, just for the roofs of the Ferrymen temples. Helen told me you'd save money in the long run on replacement batteries for the projectors."

"Especially if the batteries are getting run down because people are using them for community games." The lizard took a moment to think. "What about the potential impact on productivity?"

"We'd limit the operating hours to the evening, and because the Ferrymen temples are public places, the players can vote on the games and make sure nobody monopolizes the system to live a fantasy life."

"This calls for negotiations," the Ferryman said, and then shocked me by extending a leathery hand with stubby fingers for eBeth to shake. "I'm Trident."

"Pleased to meet you," the girl responded. "I have a consultant who handles all of my business negotiations. Do you mind?"

"Not at all. That's very wise of you."

I cleared my throat self-consciously, and then followed up with a fake cough to cover my embarrassment as eBeth gestured for the Hanker to approach.

"The idiot mage who threw the icicle?" Trident asked. "This is going to be highly profitable."

For some reason, I found myself warming to the Ferrymen chief.

Eighteen

"Is getting Lilith to do your work for you a good idea for a date?" I asked Bob when he came up to the bar and ordered an orange juice and an ale.

"I'm training her to replace me while I'm on Earth. MeAN Publishers has a backlog of printing to do for your team members, and we agreed not to use the kids to run the press."

"You've joined the management team?"

"They made me president," Bob said. "Art likes coming in and setting type but he doesn't have time to manage the business. The kids are smart, but they're starting school again in a few weeks. And now with the new gaming business she and Helen are planning with the Ferrymen, eBeth has less free time than any of us. Anyway, Lilith was my first hire."

"I don't know if mixing business and romance is wise."

"You mean the way you proposed to your second-in-command, with whom you also started a tourism business and this café?"

"Touché," I said, pushing him the tankard of ale and the glass of juice. "Tell Lilith that one is the limit while she's operating heavy equipment."

"Your English is deteriorating, Mark," Bob said. "Heavy equipment refers to excavators and bulldozers, stuff like that."

"I carried that letterpress in here, and believe me, it's heavy equipment," I retorted. "How long will you be staying on Earth?"

"Just for the length of the tour. I'm going to use the time to make sure all the legal paperwork is in place to let Donovan run The Portal in my name. I already told him he can give up his apartment and move into my house."

"That's a valuable perk."

"It's tough holding onto good restaurant help on Earth, thanks to you. I still won't be surprised if he tells me next year that he wants to go work on some alien resort like the rest of your former employees. Young people like to travel."

"Tourism is the lifeblood of the portal network," I reminded him.

"Evening, Bob," Paul said, climbing onto a stool. "Have you finished the proofs for my safety valve catalog?"

"Monos is still working on the final set of woodcuts, and Art is coming in to set the type tomorrow," Bob said. "I'd love to hang around and chat, but my date is waiting."

"Cheap date," Paul observed, after the ex-policemen took the drinks and returned to the printing press, where Lilith was cautiously turning out pamphlets for the apothecary business at about a third of the speed Bob could achieve. "Is he really making her do his work?"

"It's paid training," I explained. "She's the latest hire for MeAN Publishers. Between you and Kim, they're getting their money's worth out of that press."

"The boy does a great job with the blockcuts. He's got a future as an industrial artist if he wants it."

"Why safety valves?" I asked, setting a tumbler of single malt in front of him.

"You know, to keep the boilers from exploding."

"I meant, why have you started manufacturing them?"

"I know what you meant, Mark. You still can't tell when somebody is poking fun at you. And I haven't started manufacturing safety valves yet."

"But the catalog…" I protested.

"When I get orders, then I'll manufacture the valves. I figure it's a natural fit for the testing and certification business. Control systems are high value, and customers are willing to pay more for a name that they trust, so I shouldn't have the problems with copycats that I would get with commodity hardware. I'm also working on a steam-powered chart recorder for analytics that's generations beyond anything in use on this world."

"Then it's almost the same as magic," Helen said, taking the stool next to Paul's. "Next you'll invent a steam-powered computer."

"The control systems are a form of analog computer," Paul told her. "What are you doing away from your games?"

"I needed a break from the Ferrymen. I don't want to say that they're bad sports because they're actually great teammates, but their cultural norm is to crow about their wins to intimidate opponents. And it's frustrating that I can't get them to bet against me. They keep saying it can wait until they level up to match my character's stats."

"You're saying that they're smart."

"Too smart by half," Helen agreed. "I mean, what's the point playing one-on-one or two-on-two if you don't have a little side bet going? And they keep asking me about new games, so I'm going to have to stop by Earth and stock up."

"Why don't they go themselves?" Paul asked. "They've been there enough times in the past."

"Didn't you know they have a thing about returning to worlds where they recruited refugees for reservations? I guess some species take it the wrong way, and the Ferrymen figure better safe than sorry."

"I never got a chance to thank you for letting me play your spare mage character, Helen," I said. "It's the closest I'll ever come to doing anything magical."

"You never know, Mark. Some day in the distant future you may take Art up on his offer to port your mind into a living body, and then you can study magic for real."

I fired up my full sensor suite and did a quick scan for the Archmage before replying. "I know it might sound petty, but I'm not going to become Spot's student. I used to take him for walks."

"And you think that means you'd be lowering yourself to study under him?" Paul laughed. "Answer me this question. When you used to go on those walks, which one of you picked up the poop?"

"No comment," I muttered, and started on the latest espresso order that Athena had posted. "Anyway, I'm sorry if my lame play cost your mage levels or something, Helen."

"Doesn't work that way when the whole group wipes," she informed me. "Remember, I'm the one who built the rule set for these hybrid games."

"Have the Originals shown any interest in playing?" Paul asked.

"Zilch. I checked with Art out of curiosity, or maybe it was one of his clones, I can't really tell them apart. He said that games like that remind him of some really nasty planets he visited back when his mind was integrated in a ship."

"We need to sit down with Art and get his advice about what we're doing to this planet," I told the others. "He claims to have done everything at one time or another so maybe he'll have relevant experience. I've also put in a request to Library asking for an impact statement."

"Are you nuts?" Paul demanded. "Asking Library to evaluate anything about our conduct makes as much sense as giving yourself a sanity test!"

"You didn't see the head librarian fawning over Art," I told him. "I think we're safe doing whatever we want here as long as the Originals don't have a problem with it."

"Thanks, Mark," Athena said, picking up the two espressos I'd prepared for the romantically involved couple at the poorly lit table in the corner, another of eBeth's clever ideas. "The guy who just came in is asking to talk with the mayor."

"What did he order?"

"Nothing, yet."

"Send him over here."

I saw Paul nudge Helen and give her a 'get a load of this' eye-roll as the owner the new laundry at the other end of Main Street approached the bar.

"Mr. Mayor," he said awkwardly.

Rather than answering, I pointed to the sign Monos had carved.

"There's a one-drink minimum to talk to you?" he sputtered. "That's corrupt."

"You can talk to him for free, but you can't be in here without buying something," Paul explained.

"What's the cheapest thing on the menu?"

"Six copper will get you an ale or an espresso."

"Make it an espresso," he said, laying out six copper coins as if he were parting with his children.

"Simon," I greeted the laundryman, whose name was stenciled on his jacket, which also identified him as a member of the town's championship tug-of-war team. "What can I do for you?"

"Make the drink first," he growled.

Paul and Helen laughed out loud as I went through the process of preparing an espresso in one of the single-serving stove-top makers and presented it to Simon with a flourish.

"Now," I said, reaching under the bar and pulling out a necktie that already had the knot made. I settled the loop over my head and pulled it tight around my collar. "The mayor is in."

The laundryman took a tiny sip from his espresso and grimaced at the bitterness, but he didn't ask for a sweetener, probably out of fear that it cost extra. Then he reached inside his jacket and produced a copy of the construction plan for the Main Street water district. He jabbed at the schedule of fees with a stubby finger.

"What do you call that?" he asked. "I thought that the Originals were paying for the water system and road construction."

"They are, but there's a connection fee for users which will pay for your meter."

"I don't need one," Simon said. "I'm running a laundry, not a laboratory."

"It's a usage meter, so that the new utility can bill each customer for the water they consume rather than charging everybody the same amount."

"But you just said that the Originals are paying!"

"For construction, which is incredibly generous of them, but there will be some minor ongoing maintenance costs, like monitoring the water quality and keeping the system in good repair. It wouldn't be fair to ask the Originals to pay forever."

"But you're saying that I have to pay four silver for this connection now, and I won't even see a drop of water for another six months."

"Look at the schedule," I told him, flipping forward two pages in the construction plan. "The first phase is digging up Main Street and installing the water main and connections. The second phase is preparing the road bed and drainage, and the third phase is paving the surface with cobblestones. Springfield Drillers has already started a new town well on the public land behind the Ferrymen's temple, and we've issued a request-for-proposals to get bids on the water tower. I've never seen a municipal project move forward so quickly."

"So you're saying I pay now for a connection to a water tower that hasn't been built yet, and when the water finally does start flowing, you'll charge me an as-of-yet undetermined amount to use it?"

"How much time do you spend pumping water every day?" Paul asked him.

"More than I'd like," Simon admitted grudgingly. "Those men you employ are hard on their clothes, and none of them do their own laundry."

"And how long do you think that basement well of yours is going to last before you have to dig deeper?"

"I already spread my work through the day because my neighbors complain that I'm lowering the water table."

"Town water is going to keep you in business," I predicted boldly. "If I were you, I'd be planning on expanding as more people move here. If you don't have enough cash to pay for the meter all at once the town is offering an installment plan, but you have to sign up before the work begins. If you wait until after the road is finished and you want a connection, it will cost at least thirty silver, if not more."

"That's extortionate," Simon objected.

"Think about it. How fair would it be for the town to pay the bill to dig up a section of the road because you couldn't plan ahead?"

The laundryman took another sip of his espresso, which had cooled significantly while we argued, and then downed the remainder in one go.

"I'll have to talk it over with my wife," he said, getting to his feet and picking up the plan. "She sort of manages the household finances."

"My door is always open," I called after my constituent as he slumped out of the café. Then I swept his six copper off the bar and deposited it in the cash box.

"No tip," Helen observed.

"People hold different views about tipping the owner," I told her. "I don't take it personally."

"Are you really going to buy the water meters from that outfit in the provincial capital rather than giving the order to me?" Paul demanded, pushing his tumbler forward for a refill. "I'd cut you a quantity discount."

"They make all of the water meters for the aqueduct system and they've been around for hundreds of years," I told him. "I'm afraid if you supply the meters, people will argue about their bills."

"Here comes another one," Helen observed as a nervous looking woman made her way towards the bar. "She just opened that 'Candles and Candy' boutique next to the Chinese restaurant."

"Does she make the candles or the candy on site?" Paul asked.

"No. I stopped in to talk to her and she has suppliers all over. She already has a store at the spaceport."

"Mr. Mayor?" the boutique owner addressed me.

I pointed at the sign.

"Of course," she said, fumbling in her handbag for her change purse. "I'll have a mint tea."

"Love your store," Helen spoke across Paul. "Especially the candles."

"The apple-scented bath candle," the woman said, recognizing Helen right off. "You were my second customer. Helen, right?"

"And you're Harmonia. We're both H's."

"And I'm Mark," I said, presenting her with a mismatched tea cup and saucer. Next I spooned a healthy amount of dried mint into a strainer that fit into the individual serving ceramic teapot with a chip out of the spout, and topped it off with boiling water before setting it on the bar. "That will be seven copper. How can I help you?"

"I grew up in town before moving to the capital and eventually going into business," Harmonia explained while she sorted through her change and paid. "My parents have been writing me every month about how the town is growing, and then my father announced he was retiring from the barbering business. I think he misses bleeding people for their health."

"You can blame the local apothecaries for that," Paul told her.

"So I've heard. My parents could have converted the shop back into living space, but they already have a big apartment on the second floor with more room than they need. They didn't want strangers running a business on their first floor, so my mom started pestering me to open a second store here to see how it goes. They aren't charging rent."

"Hard to fail in retail if your overhead costs are zero," I observed. "Are you worried about the impact of the road construction? I assure you that once they start digging, it will be over sooner than you can imagine."

"No, I'm here about streetlights. I've been meditating for years and I want to try starting a group here, but the way everybody works, it would have to be at night."

"And you don't want people coming into town without streetlights when the days get shorter."

"Especially after the digging starts," she added.

"Streetlights are one of my three priorities as mayor," I told her. "We have a meeting scheduled on that very subject a week from Tuesday. I was going to print up a batch of fliers and have them delivered to every store and residence on Main Street on Friday."

"Why are you waiting?"

"If I announce it too early, people will forget."

"Is there something I can do to prepare?" Harmonia asked.

"You could talk to your neighbors about the options," I told her. "Unlike the water system and the road work, the capital investment for streetlights is low, but the ongoing maintenance cost is high. We'll almost certainly use liquid fuel lanterns which will have to be lit and extinguished each night. One option is to attach them directly to the structures on Main Street, perhaps every other house on alternating sides, and collect a small fee from everybody who benefits."

"Would it save much if the homeowners agree to take care of their own lantern?"

"It's not a trivial task, to lower a lantern, check the fuel, light or extinguish it, and raise it back up. And the glass needs to be cleaned regularly as well. But talk to your neighbors and we'll see."

"The Ferrymen already agreed to let us put photovoltaic panels on the temple roofs to recharge batteries for gaming equipment," Helen said. "Why not do the same for streetlights?"

"Maybe someday we will, but I think we should see how introducing computer games in the Ferrymen temples works out before we go any further with modern technology."

"Blah, blah, blah," Pffift announced his presence, climbing on the last open barstool. "If you're going to start casting stones at technology, you better take a long look in the mirror first."

"I'm aware that I am the product of more than a chance encounter between a sperm and an egg," I responded to the Hanker stiffly. "We're talking about the inhabitants of Reservation, not me."

"Did the Ferrymen chase you out too?" Helen asked Pffift.

"Nobody chases me out of anywhere. I left because everybody voted to play some weird game that involved driving vehicles through an unending series of left turns. I couldn't even cast an ice sheet spell to crash the competition."

"And what did the Ferrymen make of it?" I asked out of curiosity.

"The lizard-men loved it. If I could come up with a way of disguising useful work as a game, I'd foist it on them and retire a trillionaire."

"eBeth always liked racing games," I told him. "The truth is, I prefer them to any of the monster killing stuff myself, but in the end it's not very much fun playing when you know what's going to happen before it happens."

"You don't have to cheat and look at the code," Helen told me.

"It's part of my nature," I explained. "I never could get excited about games or magic. If you really want a challenge, try predicting the weather on Earth."

"Are you hanging around Reservation just to play games?" Paul asked the Hanker.

"Sue will kill me if I miss her wedding and she'll be back any week now. Can't an alien get a drink around here?"

"Sorry, Pffift," I said, drawing him an ale. "I'm trying a new world tomorrow if Paul is finished upgrading the cross-connection console."

"I replaced the tuner with something that's a little easier to control, but I'm not happy with the look of the synthetic jewels in the circuit," my technical specialist said. "Some of them have obvious microfractures, but Art told me that's normal with age."

"You're talking about the synthetic jewels I picked up from that listening outpost that the Originals abandoned eons ago?" the Hanker asked.

"They're the key to the whole thing. Art knows how to make them, but it would take him hundreds of years to bootstrap the technology base required, and that's starting from the latest Library tech. The Originals are really that far ahead of us. He'd need almost the same level of technology just to inspect the synthetic jewels we have to make sure they're safe."

"That puts the kibosh on eBeth's plans," I said. "If this world checks out as safe, she wanted me to bring her for a visit to make up for our earlier debacle."

"Art said that the worst that can happen is the cross-connection won't open," Paul said. "It can't dump you out midway. He mentioned something about going along the next time you take a short trip just to get a feel for what it's like."

"Alright," I conceded. "I'll take a week to do my usual assessment, and if everything looks good, Art and eBeth can return with me and we'll make a day of it."

Nineteen

"How was it?" eBeth asked hopefully when I entered the café. She and her partners were just finishing up a meeting with Bob, who was back from his visit to Earth. Pffift was at the next table over, huddled with the Ferrymen chief and doubtlessly up to no good.

"Unxia is a jewel of a world," I told her. "The oxygen level in the atmosphere is just a percent or two higher than Earth, the gravity is around ten percent lower, and despite a lack of interstellar spaceships, their technology will put them in the top quintile of League worlds should they accept membership. They're also open to immediate trade, so we should invite Pffift along."

"Do I need to bring lunch?" eBeth asked.

"You want to go right now?"

She looked at Art, who shrugged. "Sure. I'll make a couple of sandwiches and you talk to Pffift."

By the time I managed to pry the Hanker away from his new business buddy, eBeth was ready with a picnic basket. I hoped she had included something crunchy for me.

"You're sure that their only contact with other worlds has been via the portal system connection the Originals gave them?" Pffift asked.

"Yes, and they were one of the last planets to be added. When they visited with other species on the system they were treated like country bumpkins, and the only things they have to show for their efforts are a few tourist trinkets that didn't rise to the standard of commercial freight. Ironically, their whole portal system experience put them off developing interstellar capabilities. If everything works out, yours will be the first starship to visit."

"But thanks to the portal, they must have knowledge of what more advanced civilizations have achieved," eBeth pointed out. "That and millions of years to work with would have put them pretty far ahead of us."

"As I said, their technology is well-advanced, but the Unxians have never known the goad of healthy competition," I told her. "One of the reasons the League tolerates species like the Ferrymen and the Hankers is that their activities keep everybody else on their toes."

"Thank you," Pffift said, choosing to take my words as a compliment. "What are we waiting for?"

"Let me grab a box of universal translators from the basement and reprogram them so that the Unxians will be able to understand eBeth. Their heads are rather large, so I'll need to bring the wire adapters."

"How long will that take?" the girl asked. "You can always translate for me if I really need to say something."

"It only takes a few seconds for me to add the new language," I told her. "Meet you upstairs."

Paul was waiting by the cross-connection console when I caught up with the group on the second-floor landing. "Everybody ready?" he asked. "I'm only going to charge half as much for this trip because you've already been there and I don't have to change any of the settings."

"Peter is going to kill me for going without him," eBeth said. "Why did he have to drive the bus to the capital today?"

"We're establishing a regular once-a-week service," Paul told her. "It was your boyfriend's idea, not mine."

"Wait," Pffift said as I opened the portal. "I have to use the facility."

"We're stepping through into a visitor center. I'm sure they have a bathroom."

"Library's visitor center didn't have a bathroom," the Hanker pointed out. "Besides, it would make a bad first impression."

"There goes Spot," eBeth said, and sure enough, I caught a glimpse of the Archmage's tail disappearing through the portal. I didn't recall inviting him, but I knew better than to say anything.

"We can't leave him there alone, Pffift. There's no knowing what he might do. Paul can reopen the portal and send you through after you've taken care of your business."

"Don't sell them anything without me," the Hanker called after us as I followed Art and eBeth through the portal. It closed behind me with an odd ripping sound and the faint smell of ozone.

I glanced at eBeth, who was too busy fiddling with her ear cuff translator to have noticed the problem, but Art caught my eye and flashed me a thumbs down. The Archmage appeared to be blissfully unaware that anything had gone wrong with the cross-connection between portal networks, and was posing with muzzle raised high so that the natives could admire his faux brandy cask.

The same group of Unxians who accompanied me back to the visitor center when I returned to Reservation had apparently been so excited about the prospect of meeting an Original that they simply waited there for my return. The natives bore a slight resemblance to baby elephants that had learned to walk upright, and their arms were disproportionately short for their height by most standards, probably the evolutionary result of being equipped with a long trunk. The youngest member of the Unxian welcoming party had already put that appendage to work rubbing Spot's belly.

"We have one more coming, if the portal functions properly," I announced in the click-tongue spoken by the natives. "I brought along these translation devices so you'll be able to understand the other members of my party."

"I volunteer to be first," the largest of the Unxians said immediately. "Will it be painful?"

"No surgery involved," I promised. "The actual translation device is the silver medallion on the end, and its only function is to render English into Unxian. The rest of the hardware is just a crude headset to let me position the translator near one of your ears."

"Is it a disposable version of the pendant translator the Original is wearing?" asked another Unxian, pointing at Art.

"That's actually a thought-to-speech device," I explained, intentionally leaving the word 'magical' out of my description in case they were skeptics. "It allows Art to speak English."

"Can it be reprogrammed to speak our language?"

"Not by me," I admitted, glancing at Spot. If the Archmage caught my meaning, he chose to pretend he hadn't. I quickly bent the felt-padded coat hanger into a shape that would sit comfortably over the volunteer's head and made sure the device was positioned right over the opening of the ear.

"Can you understand me?" eBeth asked.

The Unxian displayed flat teeth in a broad smile at the results, and produced a torrent of clicks that the girl's ear cuff device translated to, "Yes, it's quite remarkable. Our historical records talk about such technology being common back when our portal was first connected, but none of the other species showed any particular interest in us, and we soon gave up on traveling due to the difficulties involved."

"What difficulties?" eBeth asked.

"Our atmospheric requirements for breathing, which you obviously share, are apparently the hallmark of younger species in this galaxy. We had to wear bulky spacesuits to visit most worlds, there was nothing to eat, and the advanced species treated us like a nuisance. The only really interesting conversations we had were with the Originals, and they stopped coming to visit us after a few thousand years."

"My apologies," Art spoke through his pendant. "We had become jaded with first contacts by that point in our history. We were all too happy to abdicate the chore of reaching out to new worlds to the League when it came along."

"Mark informed us that a few of you have chosen to spread your minds over large numbers of clones so you can experience the advantages of being alive, but he refused to go into details, saying that he'd never been alive himself," the Unxian said. "We've been dying with curiosity to ask why you'd go to such an effort."

"And I'd be happy to explain, but right now I need to use the bathroom," Art replied, casting his eye around the visitor center.

"It's out of order," the younger Unxian told him. "It didn't get used in such a long time that nobody noticed that the pipes had disintegrated. We only found out a short time ago when I went to use it while waiting for Mark's return."

"Is there somewhere nearby?" the Original asked.

"Let's all move outside," the leader said. "Anywhere is fine, but please spare the flowers."

"Pffift is never going to stop bragging about his prescience when he hears about this," eBeth said, falling in alongside me. "It's sure taking him a long time to get here."

"There may be a minor problem with the cross-connection to our portal network," I admitted.

"You mean we're stuck here?"

"No, not at all. Even if Paul can't fix the console, we can still go anywhere on the Original's portal network, including their current homeworld. If worst comes to worst, I'll pop through to there and arrange for a rescue ship."

"But that could take weeks and weeks," eBeth protested.

"We'll figure out something for you to eat," I reassured her. "The Unxians really are quite advanced."

"I don't care about that. You're supposed to be getting married Sunday."

"I am? I mean, I am, but a few weeks delay means nothing with our lifespans."

"To you, maybe," eBeth said skeptically. "I'm the one who promised Sue to keep you out of trouble."

We waited in the garden outside the visitor center for fifteen minutes just to make sure Pffift wasn't coming, and then I gave eBeth a tour of the local highlights while the Unxians quizzed Art with a million years of saved-up questions. Unfortunately, the Original could provide few answers since most of his memory was back on Reservation with his clones.

"What's wrong?" I asked eBeth after she and Art finished their picnic lunch. "I'd like to think that I know a little about human tourism by this point, and the places

I've been taking you would make the "A" list on any world. You're barely even looking."

"I'm worried about Sue and Peter," she confessed. "I can't just pretend everything is normal when we won't know until we get back to the visitor center whether or not we can return today."

"You can stop worrying," Art told her. "We can't"

"What!"

"I didn't want to say anything that would spoil your enjoyment, but it seems that I had it backwards. Now that you know we aren't getting back in a hurry, you can focus on the here and now."

"That doesn't make any sense at all," the girl objected.

"Sorry," Art said. "It was the Archmage's idea."

I looked over at the dog, who had snuck another sandwich out of the picnic basket and was eating it without removing the wax paper.

"Bad, Spot," I admonished him. "What if it takes the Unxians a day or two to synthesize something for eBeth?"

"The Archmage says not to worry," Art told me. "He suggests we open his cask."

"Well, a drink might help with the stress, but the nutritional value is low."

"He says it's a surprise."

I looked more closely at Spot, who was wearing the most self-satisfied grin I'd ever seen on any creature's face, dog or man. eBeth approached him and unbuckled the cask, then gave it an experimental shake. There wasn't any sound, which seemed unlikely unless the Archmage had used telekinesis to fill it with brandy or ale so completely that there was no empty space for sloshing around. I made a mental note to weigh the kegs and check the brandy bottles when we got back home.

"How do I open it?" the girl asked.

"Bring it over here," Art said. The Original set the cask between his knees, gripped it with one clawed hand, and began running the sharp point of a talon around and around one end of the cask.

"Are you scribing a knock-out?" I asked. "I could do a neater job with my plasma cutter if Spot wants it repaired afterwards."

"The Archmage says that it's better to eschew technology in close proximity to magic," Art replied. His claw made a faint scratching sound as it went over the same cut again and again, until finally the flat piece came free and he was able to lever it out of the cask.

"Wood shavings?" I asked. "Big surprise, Spot. I hope you've got better taste in wedding presents or Sue is going to stop making you treats."

Art inserted a couple of claws into the cask and fished around in the shavings before withdrawing a pair of bronze cylinders lashed together with a cord.

"What are those?" eBeth asked.

I stared in disbelief, never having seen so much wealth in one place in my life.

"Retrieval nets," the Original whispered through his pendant. "These are the main reason we invested millions of years developing a method to transfer ourselves into living bodies so we could learn magic. Just one of these cylinders would buy you a luxury resort moon."

"This is perfect," I said when I finally recovered my voice. "eBeth and the Archmage can return to Eniniac and take the portal to Earth. The next time one of my team members pops through with a tour group or to do a bit of internet shopping, you'll be home free."

"What about you and Art?" eBeth asked.

"We'll be fine here. Pffift wants to visit anyway, so I'll just write out the exact galactic coordinates before you go and he'll come as soon as he can."

"The Archmage says we can go Dutch," Art announced.

"Are you sure?" I asked Spot. He ignored me and started munching on the last sandwich.

"He's sure," the Original said. "And the base crystals aren't on Eniniac."

"They're on Reservation?"

"On Earth. The Regent didn't want to put too much temptation in Pffift's way so she packed the crystals in crates and sent them to Earth labeled as furniture for your wedding present. They're probably in the basement of your old restaurant."

"Bob didn't mention anything."

"Maybe he's better at surprises than you are," eBeth said.

I explained the situation to the Unxians and promised that I would return again with Pffift and more of Art's clones at the first opportunity. The leader offered me the honeymoon suite at a hotel run by his family and wished me luck on my nuptials. Then, following Spot's instructions, Art and I each took one of the cylinders. The dog jumped up, putting his paws on my shoulders, and nodded for the girl to do the same with the Original. The Unxians must have thought that we looked like the most mismatched dance partners in history.

"Hold it over your head with the nozzle pointed up and slowly depress the plunger," Art continued to relay the Archmage's telepathic instructions. "The web will surround you both naturally, but you'll have to pick up your feet for total containment."

"One at a time?" I asked.

Spot snorted in my ear.

"Yes," Art said. "Ready?"

I cranked my data recorder up to the highest bit rate to capture the experience, held the cylinder over my head like the Statue of Liberty, and slowly depressed the plunger. A fine spray of an inky black substance cascaded down about my arm and formed a shroud around the Archmage and myself. I felt Spot's body shift as he lifted a hind leg, then he transferred his weight to the other side. I did the same, and the essence of teleportation, or whatever the mages call the retrieval web, knit itself together. Suddenly, we were somewhere else.

"Break glass in case of emergency," I said out loud, and drove one of my elbows backwards. The crystal shattered easily, but we were still enclosed in a large wooden crate. I punched through carefully with a stiff finger, in case we were stacked next to the crate containing eBeth and Art, but I only encountered something soft and round that gave way easily. A quick scan showed me the side of the crate with the fewest fasteners, and fortunately the wood was strong enough that it didn't splinter into a mess. I forced the lid free and found myself buried to the neck in used tennis balls.

"Tell Art that I see their crate and I'll have them out in a minute," I said to Spot. "Pffift must have left the base crystals with his grandson, who stuck them in the back of the tennis ball warehouse and promptly forgot about them.

Twenty

"Nervous?" eBeth asked as she straightened my tie.

"AI don't get nervous," I told her. I checked my encounter suit systems versus the default settings and quickly shut down the facial tic that had given me away.

"Right, and AI don't lie either," eBeth said sarcastically. "You can't be worried that she's going to stand you up. Sue is crazy about you."

"Maybe she's better now." I grabbed eBeth's shoulders and stared into her eyes to better detect a falsehood. "You don't think she went away for treatment, do you? To get over me, I mean?"

"Relax, Mark. You have the pre-wedding jitters. She'll be here, Kim will take the plastic wrap off the buffet, everything will work out fine. Our mistake was coming early."

"You didn't see this place the last time I was here, it was just a giant empty dome. Maybe we should have had the wedding in the backyard."

"It would have been kind of embarrassing explaining to all of our friends and neighbors who think you're already married why you were having a do-over," eBeth reminded me. "Besides, your head librarian seems so proud of the new visitor center. She gave me a tour while you were hiding in the bathroom having a nervous breakdown."

"I was not hiding in the bathroom, I just wanted to make sure everything was prepared. And I never saw the

231

head librarian wearing a human encounter suit before today. They must be having a sale on the things somewhere."

"Oh, look. Art is here and he brought friends."

"I need a drink," I muttered, plastering on a smile to greet the Originals. "Art, I'm glad you could make it. I'm honored so many of you could come."

"One representative from each of our minds vacationing on Reservation," Art informed me. "It's not every day we get to see such a wonderful pair of artificial intelligences getting married. Where's the beautiful bride?"

"Ixnay on the idebray," eBeth hissed at the Original, but she was too late to stop a fresh wave of anxiety from washing over me. Then Paul arrived and handed me his drink, which I gulped down greedily.

"It's wasted if you don't enable your inebriation algorithm," he reminded me.

"You are NOT getting loaded before your wedding," eBeth said, shattering my last hope for making it through the ceremony in one piece. Then I felt a hand on my shoulder, and my encounter suit went from the edge of fight or flight to perfectly relaxed.

"Easy, Mark," my mentor cautioned me. "You were getting a little too human there. I've hacked into your maintenance system and tweaked all of the settings. Sorry I didn't arrive earlier."

"Just a little keyed up," I told him. "Sue's late."

"Actually, we're all early," eBeth said. "She's probably still getting into her dress. Don't you know it's bad luck to see the bride before the wedding?"

"AI don't believe in luck," I said reflexively.

"Hors d'oeuvre?" Justin asked, making the rounds with a tray.

"About time," I grumbled, selecting a cucumber slice with some sort of cherry tomato pinned on top with a decorative toothpick, and then wondered what I was going to do with it. Fortunately, eBeth took it out of my hand and passed it to Art, as if we had planned the whole exchange.

"One hundred percent improvement," Pffift declared, completing his own round of the visitor center. "I see the head librarian took my advice about the knee-wall, the landing field, and the furniture. You should sit before you fall down, Mark."

"All better now," I told him. "Where are your wives?"

"Do I look like a dominant male who keeps his women under lock and key?" the Hanker retorted. "My guess is that they're either on my ship or shopping somewhere."

"But I made out the invitation and got the RSVP," eBeth protested. "Sue told me to invite them."

"I didn't want to say anything, but they find humanoid bodies aesthetically objectionable," Pffift said. "It's worked out rather well for me."

"Next time you see them, please explain that checking off 'will attend' is a form of a contract."

"Saul," I greeted the president of Reservation's council of spaceports. "I'm glad you could make it."

"I would have jumped at the chance to see the mysterious homeworld of the League's artificial intelligence even if you weren't getting married," he said. "Nice dome. Is this the whole place?"

The head librarian elbowed her way around me to reply. "We're working on a complex to host students and researchers who wish to visit Library. So far, the visitor center is the only section that's pressurized, but if you come back next month the dormitories should be finished.

233

We're just waiting on a shipment of furniture," she concluded, giving Pffift a sharp look.

"It's on the way," he said. "You should have ordered standard sizes rather than supplying your own dimensions for everything. Just because a mattress factory accepts custom orders doesn't mean that they're going to drop everything to fill them."

"You said we'd get a discount for one-stop shopping," the head librarian shot back in an accusatory tone.

"I meant you should have ordered the Hanker furnishings from a Hanker factory, the human furnishings from Reservation, the Ferrymen furnishings from whoever they have making their stuff for them, like that. You ordered everything for hundreds of species from the one place."

"Back on Earth we kept a supply of air mattresses at the police station for disasters," Bob said, appearing with Lilith at his side. "You can adjust the firmness for sleeping, and if there's a flood, they float. Regular mattresses just soak through and go right to the bottom."

"Thank you for coming, Bob, Lilith," I welcomed them. "You didn't happen to see Sue hanging around the portal back on Reservation waiting to make her entrance?"

"Helen was going to help her with the veil after sending us through," Lilith said. "They'll bring the children and the dog with them."

"So the children are going to find out that we were never really married," I said in dismay. "I wanted to set a good example."

"You did, Mark," eBeth assured me. "I explained to them that artificial intelligence follows a different set of rules about these things. They don't think any less of you and Sue for living in sin."

"I love your outfit," Lilith said to the girl.

"Thank you. Sue bought the fishnet stockings and the tuxedo top on Earth for me, and I had the boots made at the new place on Main Street."

I heard the head librarian say to herself, "Cue the organ," and then the music of Handel's 'Allegro Maestoso' swelled from hidden speakers. All heads turned to the portal, and my bride-to-be entered, practically floating on a cloud of white silk. Naomi walked three steps behind her, carrying the train, followed by Monos, red-faced and fidgeting with his necktie. Then Spot made his grand entrance wearing a top hat, with a cape draped over his back. Finally, Helen stepped through, closing the portal behind her.

"Aren't we missing something?" eBeth whispered in my ear as the processional approached.

"The rings!" I exclaimed, but whatever tweaks my mentor had made to my encounter suit prevented me from going into a panic. "Paul," I whispered. "Where are the rings?"

"Right here," he said, waggling his pinky in my face to display the two gold bands.

"Classy," Bob muttered, and rolled his eyes at Lilith. I had the sudden intuition that it wouldn't be long before the pair of them followed in our footsteps.

"Not the rings," eBeth said, her voice rising. "The preacher, or the justice of the peace. You know, somebody to perform the ceremony."

"I thought Sue was arranging everything," I said, unable to look away from my approaching bride.

"I can do it," Pffift offered. "I'm a ship's captain, you know."

"I think that only works if you're on your ship," Bob told him.

"I'll be performing the ceremony at Sue's request," the head librarian informed us. "I wrote it myself."

I didn't know if I was relieved or frightened, and I couldn't help wondering if paying for the head librarian's encounter suit had been part of the deal. Now that I thought about it, Sue had asked me about the cost of encounter suits a few months back, though I hadn't been able to help her as mine had been supplied by Library's Observer service.

"Everybody other than Mark, Paul and the head librarian should go sit, I mean, stand over there," eBeth announced. "Give them some room."

"Why?" Pffift enquired. "At Hanker weddings the close friends and family of the new bonded pair show their support by removing their clothes and—"

"Don't want to hear it," eBeth interrupted. "And the reason we have to make room is so that Peter can take pictures."*

Sue was only ten steps away at this point, and I stood waiting for her, an idiotic grin on my face. I caught the edges of a tight-beam infrared transmission flashing past my shoulder, and Paul immediately stopped slouching. I traced the beam back to Stacey and sent her my thanks.

Sue's first words to me after a two month absence were, "How are you holding up?"

"Better now," I told her honestly. "It's a beautiful dress."

"And your tie is crooked," she said, straightening it for me. "You must have been playing with it again."

"I was worried you had a change of heart," I admitted. "I know I'm no great prize."

"And what you don't know would fill a library," the head librarian interrupted.

236

Naomi smoothed the long train of the dress behind Sue, and then went to stand with Monos at the front of where our guests had spread out in an arc so everybody would have an unobstructed view. Peter was moving around constantly, taking pictures from different angles with the digital camera we used for passport photos, and I saw him whisper something to Helen, who came up and stood by Sue's side.

"I know you didn't plan on a maid of honor, but Peter says the photos were out of balance," Helen said.

"Welcome to the first official event at Library's visitor center," the head librarian commenced. "Before we begin, I want to thank everybody who participated in making this new complex a reality, especially Pffift for his constructive criticism, and Saul of Reservation for pointing out that such a facility was needed. I never imagined it would result in a new revenue stream for Library, and I want to thank Mark and Sue for choosing us as their venue for this happy occasion."

"I'm paying for this?" I sent to Paul on our private channel. He replied with a shrug.

"When two artificial intelligences decide to share their lives together, it means more than just agreeing to set aside storage capacity to back up each other's memories and establishing a joint account at Library," the head librarian continued. "Some say that love can only be the result of a failed error correction mechanism, but I like to believe that certain sentients are made for each other. Having my own private sources of information about who made Mark and Sue, I think I can safely say that's the case here."

During the head librarian's significant pause, I heard Monos whisper to Naomi, "What's the old lady talking about?"

"Engineering, I think," the girl whispered back. "We can ask Mark later."

"Sue and Mark, please take one step out and face each other," the head librarian instructed us. "Do you have rings?"

Paul pulled the rings off his pinky and deposited them in the head librarian's hand. She glanced at them and then gave the smaller ring to me and the larger to Sue.

"Do you, Mark, take this AI who calls herself Sue, to share in your burdens and joys and build together a better universe?"

"Yes," I said, choking up on the word.

"And do you, Sue, take this AI who calls himself Mark, to protect him from self-doubt and keep him on the straight and narrow?"

"I do," Sue replied.

I let out a great sigh of relief.

"You may place the rings on each other's fingers," the head librarian told us.

I held Sue's ring between the thumb and forefinger of my right hand, and then drew a blank as to which of her fingers it went on. Before I could start searching Wikipedia, Sue coached me through the procedure by wiggling the appropriate digit and moving her pinkie and middle finger away. Then she took my own left hand in her own and placed the ring on my finger. I heard a number of the guests with lungs let out a sigh.

"By the power vested in me by Library's board of trustees, I now pronounce you a local area network."

"What?" I demanded.

"I thought a little humor might go over well, but some sentients—" the head librarian left the sentence hanging. "By the power vested in me by Library's board of trustees, I now pronounce you husband and wife. You may kiss the bride."

I lifted Sue's veil and my processors almost melted under the light of her shining eyes. She closed them as I leaned in, leading me to shut my own eyes in imitation, which proved to be a mistake as we didn't have that much practice in formal kisses and I ended up planting one on her nose. Next time we get married, I'll have to remember to enable my inertial guidance system.

The guests produced a hearty round of applause all the same, and then they surged forward to congratulate us. I kept a wary eye on Pffift to make sure his clothes remained on, and I heard my wife asking everybody to wait for a minute as she had something she wanted to share.

"Mark," she said, keeping a tight hold on my hand. "If you could have anything in the universe, what would it be?"

I struggled for a microsecond with eBeth's oft repeated advice never to go with my first instinct because it was sure to be wrong, then decided to ignore it this once. "You?"

"You already have me. What else?"

Now she really had me because I didn't have a clue. I considered and dismissed several possibilities before defaulting to the most popular answer given by contestants in galactic beauty contests. "Universal peace?"

Spot groaned out loud and covered his ears with his paws, pushing up his top hat. The other guests shifted into more comfortable positions as if they were settling in for a game of twenty questions, so I decided to just tell the truth.

239

"I don't know, Sue. I was hoping that you could tell me what I want from now on."

"Guess again," she instructed.

A magic show, my mentor prompted over our private channel.

I crossed the fingers of my free hand behind my back and said, "A magic show?"

Our guests gave me another brief round of applause, and then Sue asked everybody with a sensor suite to turn it off, as active technology could interfere with her wedding present to me. Justin and Kim rolled out a large cabinet finished in lacquer, and Helen brought a chair and sat me down just a couple of steps in front of the cabinet. Everybody else retreated behind me, and Spot and eBeth came forward. The Archmage jumped up, putting his front paws on the cabinet, and I have to admit that he looked the part of the magician in his top hat and cape.

eBeth made a sweeping arm gesture that I interpreted as meaning, 'Look at the cabinet,' and then pulled open the doors. The interior was empty, which she demonstrated by getting inside herself and then climbing out again, bouncing and sticking her arms out this way and that the whole time. Something told me that Peter was busy capturing it all with the camera. Then Spot gave a sharp bark and eBeth closed the doors again. Finally, the two of them rotated the cabinet through three hundred and sixty degrees.

"The Archmage says, 'I will create as I speak,'" Art informed us through his pendant. Then Spot hopped down and hit the cabinet a few solid thwacks with his wagging tail. eBeth did another bounce and arm extension, then opened the cabinet doors.

A boy who looked to be about the same age as Monos peeked out from the cabinet, focused on me, and asked, "Are you my mentor?"

I turned my sensor suite back on and immediately saw that the boy was an artificial intelligence wearing a small encounter suit. Somehow, he had my wife's eyes.

"That's where I've been for two months," Sue told me. "I convinced Library to make an exception to the adults-only rule for encounter suits and spawned a new process using our core backups. He's been waiting to meet you."

As our offspring climbed out of the cabinet, I rose from the chair and then went to my knees before him, to bring our eyes to the same level. "I'm Mark," I said. "What's your name?"

"Ben," he replied, "But you can change it if you want."

"Don't change anything," I breathed, pulling him towards me in a bear hug, and I sensed that all of the guests were moving away to the buffet to give us a little privacy. For some reason, I picked Pffift's voice out of the subdued murmur of conversation as he told the head librarian, "I saw that trick done once on Rigel Six." What a liar.

Sue knelt beside me and put her arms around both of us, then asked in a teasing voice, "Did I do good?"

"Spot and the Originals can keep their transportation crystals and telepathy," I replied honestly. "This is the best magic ever."

Postscript

"Those retrieval webs were for an emergency!" the Regent of Eniniac blasted at her husband via their telepathically linked crystal balls. "Do you have any idea how much it costs to hire a team of mages to sing in relays at a base crystal for year after year until it gives up its essence?"

"It was an emergency," the Archmage protested. "You wouldn't want Mark to be late for his own wedding, would you?"

"But I intended them as presents to show how much we value our connection with Library. I've set aside a nice silver service for Pffift to bring them on his next trip as a late gift, but I doubt the AI will get much use out of it."

"Art can't stop talking about the experience," Spot boasted. "He keeps going on about the warp and weft of the space-time continuum being within their grasp."

"Don't tell me you broke the cross-connection on purpose to have an excuse to use the retrieval webs!" The Regent let out a long sigh. "I should have known better than to trust you with them in the first place. Don't expect any more home-baked biscuits from me, Mr. Archmage."

"Wait! You have it all wrong. I did it for business reasons."

"This better be good."

"I've been studying the Hanker and he always hooks his customers in with free samples. The Originals are

242

loaded with money, and once Art tells his friends how well the retrieval webs work you'll have orders piled up for the next thousand years."

"Until they learn to sing the webs out of the crystals themselves," the Regent pointed out. "You're destroying our monopoly for short-term gains."

Spot broke into a big doggy smile and his tongue lolled out the side of his mouth. "I may have overpromised a little as to their capabilities."

"How little?" his wife demanded.

"They have perfect pitch when they sing through telepathy-to-speech pendants, but without them, let's just say you better bring ear protection. The Originals have sufficient singing talent to control the weather, but they'll never master the art of addressing lattice atoms on an individual basis, at least not in those bodies."

"They're the most patient sentients in the galaxy," the Regent cautioned her husband. "If it takes them millions of years to evolve new host bodies, they'll just try again."

"You and I will be long gone by then," the Archmage pointed out. "Nothing lasts forever."

"Did you just make that up?"

Spot considered lying, but the stakes were too high. "No, everybody on Earth says that, mainly because their stuff is junk. But I did come up with, 'Statistics quantify the improbable, magic explains the impossible,' and Art repeats it all the time. Artificial intelligences are big on statistics."

"I suppose we could get a trademark and print it on T-shirts, though I don't know who would wear them." His wife relented and gave her crystal ball a friendly lick. "How was the wedding?"

"I helped eBeth perform the old surprise-son-in-a-cabinet trick. Pffift was the only one who had seen it before, and Mark almost fell off his chair."

"Being ambushed with a child like that must be a shock," the Regent said, forgetting that she had presented the Archmage with his own offspring after dispatching him on a long and pointless diplomatic mission so she could get some peace and quiet around the palace while expecting. "Still, cabinets do have their uses."

"Speaking of which, I've commissioned the ex-policeman to start building a new cabinet for me," Spot said. "I've had an idea for a trick where I saw eBeth in half and then put her back together."

"That sounds dangerous," the Regent replied doubtfully.

"I'm not really going to saw her in half. She's going to curl up in one end of the cabinet and push a stick with her boots out the other end. Then she'll scream and shake the stick. Maybe we'll use ketchup too."

"Ketchup sounds nice. I hope you're eating well."

"You too, my love. We'll talk soon."

Visit a brighter future with my EarthCent Ambassador series. I've put together a discounted three-book bundle, **Union Station 1, 2, 3**, for readers who are just getting started.

About the Author

E. M. Foner lives in Northampton, MA with an imaginary German Shepherd who's been trained to bite bankers. The author welcomes reader comments at e_foner@yahoo.com.

Other books by the author:

Meghan's Dragon

Turing Test

Human Test

Date Night on Union Station

Alien Night on Union Station

High Priest on Union Station

Spy Night on Union Station

Carnival on Union Station

Wanderers on Union Station

Vacation on Union Station

Guest Night on Union Station

Word Night on Union Station

Party Night on Union Station

Review Night on Union Station

Family Night on Union Station

Book Night on Union Station

LARP Night on Union Station

Career Night on Union Station

Made in the USA
Las Vegas, NV
22 January 2021